IN THE PICTURE FANTASIES

Once Upon A Galaxy

'IN THE PICTURE' FANTASIES

Titles

Historical Hysterics

Arabian Night Jinks

Sky High

A Monster'ous Story

'Old Master' Tricks

Making Waves

A Bunch of Roses

On Your Marc O'Polo

Spying Saucers

Troy Boys

A Midsummer Night's Scream

Knights of the Square Table

A Lot of Bottle and Ship

A Scotch Frisky

Creeps get Creepier

The Fire & Brimstone Guy

Treasure Island Spoof
-
Once Upon A Galaxy

Once Upon A Galaxy

Annie G.

Published 2005 by
AgiliTyping Ltd
Distribution
39 Totteridge Lane
London N20 OHD
Tel: 020 8446 0086
Fax: 020 8449 7926
email:info@itpfscreenplays.co.uk
www.itpfscreenplays.co.uk

Agil. typing

COVER AND ILLUSTRATIONS
DAVID LOWRIE

Photograph
Marti Friedlander

Produced by:
Copyspeed Printing & Imaging (CPI)
Finchley Central, London N3 2SA
www.cpi-global.co.uk

IN THE PICTURE FANTASIES
screenplays

'IN THE PICTURE' FANTASIES
screenplays

A screenplay is a drama that is played-out on the television or cinema screen.

With a screen drama, the story moves along with the use of pictures and a change of screen brings the action into a different location; dialogue is mainly used to reveal the character of the person speaking and give background information

A screenplay makes exciting and easy reading.

If you have a story that you would like to see on film, write it as a screenplay, film the action, and you've got your own movie.

Enjoy!

Annie G.

List of screenplay terms and abbreviations end of book.

ONCE UPON A GALAXY

IN A FLASH THE CHILDREN WERE
GONE AND ALL THAT REMAINED
WAS AN EERIE EMPTINESS............
Abducted to another planet by the
Pied Piper, they meet up with ESH an
'Ever So Helpful' MOUSE.

screenplay

CAST

YOUNG FRIENDS:

James Baines (11)	aka 'Private Eye Baines'
Gemma Baines (9)	aka 'Iron Kid'
Ben Prince (11)	aka 'Brother'
Kathy Murphy (9)	aka 'Goody Goody Gumboots'

'THE PETS' POP GROUP

Teenagers

Marvin Powell	Lead singer and guitarist
Andrew Burton	Plays the guitar. Also, training to be an actor.
Pete Watson	Plays the keyboard
Denzil Taylor	Plays the saxophone
Terry Murphy	Plays the drums.
Lana Lawson	Dance backup Love-hates Andrew
Jade Tyson	Dance backup

(Overall cast in order of appearance end of screenplay)

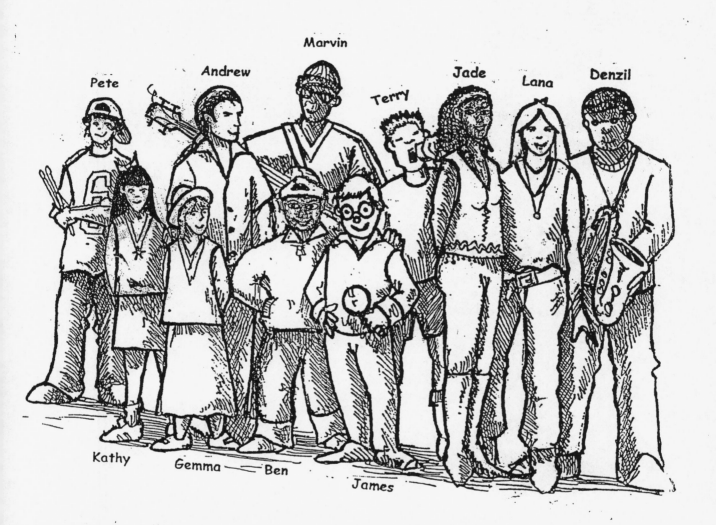

Pete
Andrew
Marvin
Terry
Jade
Lana
Denzil
Kathy
Gemma
Ben
James

'Ever So Helpful Whizmouse'
aka 'ESH'

'ONCE UPON A GALAXY'

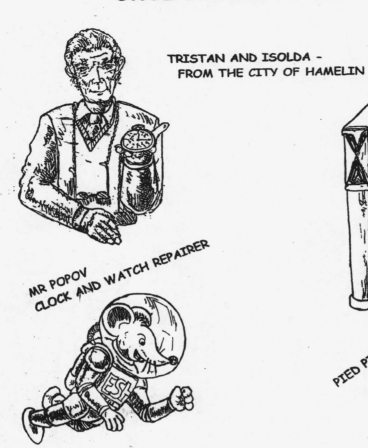

TRISTAN AND ISOLDA –
FROM THE CITY OF HAMELIN

MR POPOV
CLOCK AND WATCH REPAIRER

'ESH' EVER SO HELPFUL GALAXIAN WHIZMOUSE

PIED PIPER

HUMP RULER OF PLANET MOONA

CANDIOLLA

QUEEN DENDERRA

HORSE COWBOYS 'THE TANGLERS'

MOOKINA AND MOOKIN
BIRDS OF THE MOONSEAS

TRUNKA THE TINKER OF THE GALAXY

THE RED DRAGON

RUDI THE REINDEER

CAT QUEEN 'QUEEN MEDEA'

clapperboard

TAKE

1 2 3

production

ONCE
UPON
A
GALAXY

TAKE 1

A plague of RATS

FADE IN

CITY OF HAMELIN
Fifteenth Century

RATS ARE SCAMPERING ALONG THE COBBLED STREETS.

THEY GO AMONGST CHILDREN AT PLAY, WHO ARE RUNNING ABOUT CHASING ONE ANOTHER, BOUNCING A BALL, BOWLING A HOOP, OR TURNING A SKIPPING ROPE. THEIR HAPPY CHATTERING AND LAUGHTER CHANGES TO SCREAMS OF TERROR AS THEY DROP THEIR PLAYTHINGS AND FLEE IN ALL DIRECTIONS TO ESCAPE THE RATS.

Cut to
MARKET PLACE

THE RATS SCRAMBLE OVER STALLS PILED HIGH WITH WARES AND GOBBLE UP THE FOOD ON DISPLAY. THE STALL OWNERS STRIKE THEM WITH STAVES, BUT TO NO AVAIL.

Cut to
ROW OF HOUSES

A WOMAN, WHO IS WEARING A BONNET AND CLOAK AND CARRYING A BASKET OVER HER ARM, OPENS THE DOOR TO A HOUSE. THE RATS RUSH THROUGH THE OPEN DOOR WITH SUCH FORCE THAT SHE FALLS TO THE FLOOR. HER SCREAMS ARE STIFLED BY THE STAMPEDING RATS.

Cut to
CITY HALL

THE CITIZENS CONFRONT THE MAYOR OF HAMELIN.

    CITIZENS CHORUS: *RATS! RATS!*
                                We can't get rid of the rats!

    CITIZEN 1:   *They fight the dogs and kill the cats,*
                                And bite the babies in their cradles.

CITIZEN 2:   *And eat the cheeses out of the vats,*
                    And lick the soup from the cooks' own ladles
                    Split open the kegs of salted sprats.

CITIZEN 3:   *Make nests inside men's Sunday hats,*
                    And even spoil the women's chats
                    By drowning their speaking
                    With shrieking and squeaking
                    In fifty different sharps and flats.

CITIZENS CHORUS: *RATS! RATS!*
                    We can't get rid of the rats.

                                                              (Robert Browning)

Cut to
HILLS AND DALES

THE HAMELIN TOWN CRIER COMES INTO VIEW RINGING A BELL.

LOUD SONOROUS VOICE:

                    HEAR YE! HEAR YE!
                    THE CITIZENS OF HAMELIN
                    WILL PAY ONE THOUSAND GUILDERS
                    TO ANYONE WHO CAN RID THE CITY
                    OF THE RATS.

FADE OUT

TAKE 2

A Pied Piper

FADE IN

A WOOD

CANDIOLLA, A BEAUTIFUL GIRL, COMES INTO VIEW WALKING SLOWLY TOWARDS A TUMBLEDOWN COTTAGE. TWO THICK PLAITS OF GOLDEN HAIR FALL TO HER WAIST, HER CLOTHES ARE RAGGED, HER FEET BARE. SLUNG ACROSS HER SHOULDERS IS A STAVE, AT EACH END HANGS A PAIL OF WATER.

NEARBY, THE GIRL'S FATHER, WHO IS A WOODCUTTER, APPLIES AN AXE TO A LOG.

PIED PIPER ARRIVES ON THE SCENE. HE IS A STRANGE-LOOKING FELLOW, HIS EYES A PIERCING BLUE, HIS FEATURES SHARP. HE IS QUAINTLY CLOTHED IN A CAP FINISHED BY A LONG TAIL AND TASSEL, A TUNIC AND STOCKINGS. THE OUTFIT IS HALF RED AND HALF YELLOW. A FLUTE IS TUCKED INTO HIS BELT.

HE REMOVES THE STAVE FROM THE GIRL'S SHOULDERS.

PIED PIPER:	(*Earnestly implores*) Marry me, Candiolla - I am dying of love for you.
CANDIOLLA:	(*Shaking her head*) I shall only marry the man who can give me a grand house, fine clothes and jewels.

HAMELIN'S TOWN CRIER COMES INTO VIEW RINGING A BELL.

TOWN CRIER:	**HEAR YE! HEAR YE!** **THE CITIZENS OF HAMELIN** **WILL PAY ONE THOUSAND GUILDERS** **TO ANYONE WHO CAN RID THE CITY** **OF THE RATS.**
PIED PIPER:	If I had one thousand Guilders, would you then marry me, Candiolla?

HER REPLY IS A WHIMSICAL SMILE.

Cut to
CITY HALL

PIED PIPER IS STANDING BEFORE THE MAYOR OF HAMELIN.

THE MAYOR'S BUSHY EYEBROWS ARE ARCHED IN AMAZEMENT AS HE TAKES IN FROM TOP TO TOE PIED PIPER'S CURIOUS APPEARANCE.

MAYOR:	How is it possible for one such as you to rid our city of the rats?
PIED PIPER:	(*Singsong voice*)

'Please your Honour, I'm able
By means of a secret charm to draw
All creatures living beneath the sun
That creep or swim or fly or run
After me as you never saw!
And I chiefly use my charm
On creatures that do people harm,
The mole and toad and newt and viper
And people call me the PIED PIPER.'

(Robert Browning)

MAYOR:	(*Sternly*) Prove what you say you can do.

Cut to
DESERTED STREETS OF HAMELIN

THE CITIZENS CAN BE SEEN PEERING FROM THE WINDOWS OF THE HOUSES.

PIED PIPER IS JIGGING ALONG TO THE NOTES OF HIS FLUTE. IN RESPONSE TO ITS TUNE, HORDES AND HORDES OF RATS FROM EVERY CORNER OF THE CITY, ALL SHAPES, COLOURS AND SIZES COME INTO VIEW AND IN A MAD SCAMPERING MASS FOLLOW THE PIED PIPER AS HE JIGS ALONG.

Cut to
RIVER BANK

PIED PIPER IS JIGGING ALONG THE BANK OF THE RIVER. THE NOTES OF THE FLUTE MERCILESSLY PROPEL THE RATS FORWARD AND THEY PLUNGE PELL MELL INTO THE RIVER, LAYER UPON LAYER IN A DENSE WRIGGLING MASS AND SINK TO THE BOTTOM. AT LAST, THERE IS NOT A RAT TO BE SEEN ON THE RIVER'S GENTLY RIPPLING SURFACE.

Cut to
CITY HALL

PIED PIPER IS STANDING BEFORE THE MAYOR.

PIED PIPER:	If, you please Your Honour, the reward of one thousand Guilders.
MAYOR:	*(Jovially)* Now, what would a Pied Piper want with one thousand Guilders? We're not folks to shrink from the duty of giving you a sum for a drink. Come now! Take fifty.
PIED PIPER:	*(Insistently)* One thousand Guilders!
MAYOR:	Fifty!
PIED PIPER:	*(High pitched angry tone)* ***Folks who put me in a passion,*** ***May find me pipe in another fashion.***
MAYOR:	*(Shouting, red in the face)* Fifty Guilders!

PIED PIPER VIGOROUSLY SHAKES HIS HEAD AND DEPARTS.

Cut to
STREETS OF HAMELIN

PIED PIPER IS JIGGING ALONG THE COBBLED STREETS PLAYING HIS FLUTE. IN RESPONSE TO ITS EERIE NOTES, DOORS OF THE HOUSES BURST OPEN AND **BOYS AND GIRLS JIG OUT OF THEM.** THEY FOLLOW IN PIED PIPER'S WAKE, WOODEN CLOGS CLATTERING ON THE COBBLE STONES, HANDS CLAPPING AND VOICES CHATTERING.

CHILDREN PLAYING ON THE STREETS LET THEIR PLAYTHINGS FALL AND JIG INTO LINE ALONG WITH THE OTHERS.

Cut to
CLOCKTOWER

PIED PIPER COMES INTO VIEW JIGGING ALONG TO THE NOTES OF HIS FLUTE, FOLLOWED BY THE DANCING CHILDREN.

THE **KEEPER** HAS HIS BACK FIRMLY TO THE SHUDDERING DOOR OF THE CLOCKTOWER PREVENTING IT FROM OPENING. A **BOY AND GIRL** ARE GLIMPSED BEHIND HIM.

PIED PIPER JIGS ONWARDS, BEYOND THE CITY GATES, FOLLOWED BY THE CHILDREN UNTIL THE LAST SMALL DANCING FEET DISAPPEAR FROM SIGHT.

A **LAME BOY,** UNABLE TO CATCH UP, LOOKS WISTFULLY AFTER THEM.

FADE OUT

TAKE 3

What's ticking?

FADE IN

MR POPOV'S SHOP — NORTH LONDON

IT IS A NARROW SHOP IN A RUNDOWN PARADE, THE NAME OF THE OWNER AND TRADE AS A WATCH AND CLOCK REPAIRER, FADED.

BEN AND **JAMES** COME INTO VIEW AND ENTER THE SHOP.

Cut to
INT: SHOP

THE PROPRIETOR, A SMALL WHITE-HAIRED MAN, IS SITTING AT A BENCH LITTERED WITH BITS AND PIECES OF WATCHES AND ALL THEIR DELICATE PARTS. HE HAS A JEWELLER'S EYEGLASS TUCKED IN ONE EYE AND IS USING TWEEZERS TO PUT TOGETHER THE PARTS OF A WATCH CUPPED IN HIS HAND. BY HIS ELBOW, IS A LAMP, THE GLARE FROM ITS NAKED BULB SUPPLEMENTS THE GLOOMY LIGHT SHED BY THE BARE BULB DANGLING CROOKEDLY FROM THE CEILING.

BEN: *(Cheerfully)*
         Hi, Mr Popov! Is your phone out of order? Dad has been trying to ring you.

MR POPOV: *(Puts the receiver of the telephone to his ear)*
         The line's gone dead!

| BEN: | I've come about the pocket watch you're repairing for Dad. He'd like to put it on the stall he has in the Saturday market. |
| MR POPOV: | *(Looking around the bench)*
It's here somewhere. |

BEN SMILINGLY WAVES TOWARDS A ROW OF DUSTY SHELVES, ON THEM A JUMBLE OF CLOCKS.

| JAMES: | Who are you waving to, Bro? |
| BEN: | *(Pointing)*
The boy and girl in that clock that has 'Hamelin' on it. I always wave to them when I come in here, they look so sad. |

JAMES SHINES HIS TORCH ON THE CLOCK.

THE CLOCK IS MADE OF WOOD AND UNLIKE THE OTHERS ON THE SHELVES, IS FREE OF DUST, ITS COLOURS STRANGELY FRESH. ITS DESIGN IS THAT OF A CLOCKTOWER AS SEEN IN THE MARKET PLACE OF TOWNS IN 'OLDEN TIMES'. PAINTED ON THE CLOCK IN BOLD LETTERS IS **'HAMELIN'** AND STANDING WITHIN ITS PORTALS ARE THE FIGURES OF A **BOY AND GIRL**, THE EXPRESSION ON EACH FACE HAS AN ALMOST HUMAN SADNESS.

JAMES:	*(Jumps back and gasps)* The boy's eye blinked!
BEN:	*(Crossly)* How come wherever *you* are James, something strange happens?
JAMES:	Because I'm 'Private Eye Baines' and I pick up on anything fishy. *(His torch still lighting up the clock)* How long has this Hamelin clock been in your shop, Mr Popov?
MR POPOV:	*(Squints in the direction of the clock)* Can't recall how it ever came to be in my shop.

HE DANGLES AN ANTIQUE POCKET WATCH BY ITS CHAIN.

Here's the watch Ben! I didn't think it could be repaired, it's so old, but when I opened it up and oiled its parts, it began ticking again as good as new.

| BEN: | *(Puts the watch to his ear)*
The tick's really loud. |
| JAMES: | Let me listen!
(Puts the watch to his ear)
I hear someone crying – sounds like – |

. HE HURRIES UP TO THE 'HAMELIN' CLOCK AND SHINES HIS TORCH ON IT.

A TEAR IS ROLLING DOWN THE GIRL'S PINK CHEEK.

FADE OUT

TAKE 4

Sparks are flying

FADE IN

'MOON ROLLOVER' - PLANET MOONA

A BROAD SILVER MOON SHIMMERS OVER AN IMPRESSIVE DOME, DOMINATING THE PLANET'S ICY TERRAIN.

THE **INTERIOR OF THE DOME** IS EQUIPPED LIKE AN **AMUSEMENT ARCADE** AND LIT UP BY RIBBONS OF GLOW-WORMS THAT TRAIL OVER SPECTACULAR STALACTITES AND STALAGMITES. IT VIBRATES WITH THE SOUNDS OF BELLS CLANGING, LEVERS CLONKING, AND THE TINKLING VOICES OF **STARS,** WHO ARE PLAYING ON ROWS OF **FUN MACHINES.**

WE FOCUS ON **HUMP, THE RULER OF PLANET MOONA,** WHO IS WITH **PIED PIPER.** THE LATTER IS SITTING CROSS-LEGGED, HIS FLUTE RESTING ON HIS KNEES.

HUMP IS VERY ANGRY. FIERY SPARKS ISSUE FROM STAR-SHAPED EYES IN HIS GLASSY ROUND FACE. HIS BROAD FRAME, CLOTHED IN A WHITE ROBE EMBROIDERED WITH FLASHING CRYSTALS, IS BLAZING LIKE A CANDELABRA AS HE WOBBLES IN TEMPER. THE SILVER CROWN ON HIS HEAD, ITS CENTREPIECE A CRESCENT-MOON, IS ASKEW.

HUMP:	*(Squeals)* A sack of moonbeams was good enough last time, Pied Piper. Why now the crock of gold at the end of the rainbow?
PIED PIPER:	*(Scowling)* It's what the Red Dragon wants in exchange for the Golden Fleece.
HUMP:	*(Splutters)* The Golden Fleece! What's *that* old skin got to do with our deal?
PIED PIPER:	By putting on the fleece you can wish yourself to change into the exact likeness of somebody else. *(Drools)* I'd wish to be the image of the handsome God Anchises.
HUMP:	*(Astounded)* Why would you want to look like him?

PIED PIPER SWAYS ABOUT BASHFULLY.

	(Eyes soften to a twinkle) Oooh! Who is she?
PIED PIPER:	*(Low reverent voice)* Candiolla.
HUMP:	*(Expression amazed)* Candiolla! She's gorgeous, but why set your sights so high, Pied Piper? There are so many pretty stars in the galaxy you could twinkle with.
PIED PIPER:	*(Sadly)* I can't help myself! I've loved Candiolla way back to when she was a poor woodcutter's daughter.
HUMP:	`Beauty is in the eye of the beholder`. Look at me, Pied Piper! I'm no Anchises - *(Wobbles ecstatically)* But my Queen Denderra loves me.
PIED PIPER:	*(Miserably)* I'm only a speck in the galaxy to Candiolla, but if I was to become, *tall, dark and handsome.*

HUMP LOOKS PIED PIPER UP AND DOWN.

HUMP:	Well, for starters, you're tall —

HE TRAILS OFF LOOKING DISMAYED AT PIED PIPER'S UGLINESS.

PIED PIPER: *(Obstinately)*
I must have the Golden Fleece!

HUMP: *(Soothing tone)*
You'll have it Pied Piper.

HE PONDERS A FEW SECONDS THEN WOBBLES EXCITEDLY

I'm throwing a *'MOON-ROLLOVER' TURNOVER*
(*Throws up his arms in a dramatic gesture*)
Win yourself a galaxy! Have yourself, a Milky Way!
Candiolla will be there and I'll invite the Red Dragon.

PIED PIPER: *(Gloomily)*
The galaxy will be full of black-holes from stars that have gone bust.

HUMP: *(Gleefully)*
That's the nature of the game, Pied Piper! Evil and wickedness are so profitable.
(*Points towards the stars playing on the fun machines*)
Down below on planet Earth they look up at the stars twinkling so innocently in the galaxy.
(*Squealing laughter*)
If they only knew what was behind their twinkling.

PIED PIPER: It's said, *'The power of good triumphs over the power of evil.'*

HUMP: Want to bet on it, Pied Piper?

PIED PIPER: *(Vigorously shaking his head)*
I'm a born loser! Remember how the citizens of Hamelin played me up? By the way, how are their children doing?

HUMP LEADS PIED PIPER TO **THE CHILDREN OF HAMELIN.**

SOME OF THE CHILDREN, A BROOM IN THEIR HANDS, ARE SWEEPING UP ICICLES ON THE GROUND; OTHERS ARE POLISHING THE STALAGTITES AND STALAGMITES. THE CHILDREN'S MOVEMENTS ARE STIFF, THEIR FACES DEADPAN.

HUMP:	(Sighing) They've become weary. I need new blood to swell my workforce. Bring me some more children and we're in business Pied Piper.
PIED PIPER:	I'll flute them as far as the Selestria Platform.
HUMP:	(Wobbling in excited anticipation) Splendid! I'll send my ship to pick them up.

FADE OUT

TAKE 5

An 'Abduction'

FADE IN

JOHN BAINES'S PRINTING BUSINESS

A VAN IS DRIVEN INTO THE PARKING LOT: IT IS BROUGHT TO A HALT, AND **LLOYD PRINCE**, THE FATHER OF BEN, A HUGE 'SAMPSON' OF A MAN, ALIGHTS.

Cut to
SKY

LLOYD PRINCE LOOKS WONDERINGLY AT A **GLEAMING SAUCER SHAPE THAT IS SPINNING IN THE SKY.** IT DISAPPEARS ABRUPTLY.

HE REMOVES A TROLLEY FROM THE VAN AND WHEELS IT ONTO THE PREMISES.

JOHN BAINES IS SITTING AT A DESK SORTING THROUGH PAPERS.

SITTING ON THE OTHER SIDE OF THE DESK IS HIS DAUGHTER **GEMMA.** HER FACE HAS BEEN PAINTED INTO A FEARSOME EXPRESSION. HER DARK BROWN HAIR IS COILED INTO A THICK PLAIT THAT STANDS UP IN A RIGID POLE ON TOP OF HER HEAD. HER CLOSE-FITTING PANTSUIT HAS STUCK ON IT TWO BIG STARING EYES.

LLOYD PRINCE:	Hi, John! Somethin' really vexin' happened as I drove up. Lights flashed across the windscreen of my van, near blinded me! Came from somethin' flyin' in the sky — can't say what it was exactly.
JOHN BAINES:	Could be a U.F.O.
LLOYD PRINCE:	What's that then?
JOHN BAINES:	An unidentified flying object - believed by many to be alien craft visiting our planet.
GEMMA:	*(Stands up and says fiercely)* I'm an alien!
LLOYD PRINCE:	*(Jumps back in a merry gesture of fright)* Your outfit's really somethin', Gemma!
GEMMA:	*(Grinning)* There's a Fancy Dress disco at my school, its theme, 'Aliens from another Planet'.
JOHN BAINES:	It's time we were getting along to the school, Gemma.
	THE TWO LEAVE THE WAREHOUSE.

Cut to
ASSEMBLY HALL - KNOWALL JUNIOR SCHOOL

IT IS DECKED OUT TO LOOK LIKE THE GALAXY. COLOURED LOW LIGHTS MINGLE WITH MODELS OF THE PLANETS. A BROAD BRIGHT FULL MOON IS SURROUNDED BY GLITTERING STARS.

SOME OF THE CHILDREN WEAR GROTESQUE MASKS. OTHERS HAVE HAD THEIR FACES PAINTED. ALL OF THEM WEAR GARISH FANCY DRESS.

GEMMA ARRIVES AND JOINS HER BEST FRIEND KATHY.

KATHY'S FACE HAS BEEN PAINTED. TWO ANTENNAS STICK UP FROM HER FAIR HAIR SPRAYED WITH SILVER DUST. HER OUTFIT IS A MAUVE PANTSUIT APPLIQUED WITH SILVER STARS.

KATHY:	Is James coming to the disco, Gemma?
GEMMA:	(*Scowling*) No, thank goodness!
KATHY:	(*Disappointed*) Oh!
GEMMA:	Don't know what you see in my brother – he's a pain!

THE SCHOOL'S **HEADMISTRESS** ARRIVES ON THE SCENE, ALSO WEARING FANCY DRESS. ON HER HEAD SITS A STEEPLE SHAPED HAT, AN ANTENNA RISING FROM IT. A HOOKED NOSE HAS BEEN FIXED OVER HER OWN. THE REST OF HER OUTFIT IS A LONG BLACK CAPE THAT HAS STUCK ON IT WEIRD SYMBOLS.

HEADMISTRESS:	(*Booms*) Our disco is about to begin Aliens and 'THE PETS' pop group are here to provide the music.

Cut to

'THE PETS' POP GROUP

ANDREW AND **MARVIN** EACH HOLD A GUITAR, **DENZIL** A SAXOPHONE, **PETE** A KEYBOARD, **TERRY** SITS IN FRONT OF A SET OF DRUMS. **LANA AND JADE** ARE THE DANCERS.

ANDREW:	Hi, everyone! We call ourselves 'THE PETS' because we all live in Petunia Heights. - So here we go aliens, do your worst!

THE GROUP LAUNCH INTO A GIG:

MARVIN IS THE LEAD SINGER:

'Up, down and around we go,
As madly as can be.
We're extra terrible aliens,
And devilish company.

Spread around the agro,
Spread around the pain,
We're doing our worst together,
On an inter-galactic plane.

> *We're weird'os,*
> *We're to be feared'os,*
> *We're your worst nightmare – '*

THE CHILDREN DANCE WILDLY.

THE EERIE PIPING OF A FLUTE RISES ABOVE THE MUSIC.

PIED PIPER IS BARELY VISIBLE STANDING BESIDE MARVIN.

MARVIN:	*(Glaring at Pied Piper)* This ain't your gig, Man! Take your beat somewhere else!

THERE IS A SUDDEN TOTAL BLACKNESS AND DEAD SILENCE FOR A FEW MOMENTS.

TEACHER'S VOICES:	What's happened? – Anyone got a light?
HEADMISTRESS:	*(Shrilly)* Where's the caretaker?
CARETAKER:	*(Male voice)* Here!
HEADMISTRESS:	What's happened to the lights?
CARETAKER:	Must be a power-cut.

THE LOWLIGHTS COME BACK ON.

ALL THE CHILDREN AND THE TEENAGERS, ALONG WITH THEIR MUSICAL INSTRUMENTS, HAVE VANISHED.

THE HEADMISTRESS AND OTHER TEACHERS FRANTICALLY SEARCH THE CLASSROOMS.

ONLY AN EERIE EMPTINESS REMAINS.

FADE OUT

TAKE 6

What's sitting on the roof?

FADE IN

JOHN BAINES' BUSINESS PREMISES

JAMES AND BEN ENTER.

JOHN BAINES IS SITTING AT HIS DESK SORTING THROUGH PAPERS.

JOHN BAINES:	Now you're here to hold the fort, James, I'll pick up Gemma from the school, the disco's finishing about now.
BEN:	*(Dangling the pocket watch)* I called in to give this watch to dad.
JOHN BAINES:	He's out delivering, Ben. Should be back soon.
	HE DEPARTS.
	THE BOYS SIT EITHER SIDE OF HIS DESK.

THERE IS THE SOUND OF LOUD BLEEPING COMING FROM OUTSIDE.

THE BOYS JUMP UP AND GO OUTSIDE.

Cut to
OUTSIDE

THE BLEEPING NOISE IS ACCOMPANIED BY FLASHING RAINBOW LIGHTS COMING FROM A SPHERICAL SHAPED SPACESHIP SITTING ON THE ROOF OF THE PREMISES.

A PATH OF LIGHT EXTENDS FROM THE SHIP UNDER THE FEET OF THE BOYS. THEY VANISH FROM SIGHT.

Cut to
INT: SHIP

JAMES AND BEN ARE STARING IN WONDER AT THE PILOT.

AN EAR JUTS OUT EITHER SIDE OF THE PILOT'S HELMET AND A LONG SLIM TAIL CURLS FROM THE REAR PART OF THE SPACESUIT.

JAMES:	*(Firmly)* A MOUSE!
MOUSE:	*(Trills)* Hi!
BEN:	You talk?
MOUSE:	I'm a Whizmouse. TAPS THE LETTERS **'E S H'** THAT GLEAM ON THE BREAST OF THE SPACESUIT. ESH is my name, short for, 'Ever So Helpful.'
BEN:	*(Working it out)* E for 'Ever', S for 'So', H for 'Helpful' - That figures! My name is Benjamin, but I'm called Ben, for short.
JAMES:	Hi! My name is James.
ESH:	What's your name for short?
BEN:	Nosy!
JAMES:	*(Pushing Ben aside)* Does your name mean you help people?
ESH:	Right! I'm trailing a Pied Piper who's fluted away children from around here and is taking them to Planet Moona.
JAMES:	*(Excitedly)* Can I help you?
ESH:	You bet! That's why I landed on this roof. You're the sleuth, Private Eye Baines. Right? JAMES NODS, DUMBFOUNDED.
BEN:	*(Stoutly)* I'd also like to help!
JAMES:	*(Puts an arm around Ben's shoulders)* My assistant. *(Grins)* I'm the 'brains' and he's the 'brawn'.

BEN, TALL FOR HIS AGE AND STOCKY, PULLS UP THE SHORT SLEEVE OF HIS
SHIRT, TUCKS A HAND UNDER THE ELBOW OF ONE ARM, FLEXES HIS FIST
AND PRODUCES A SIZEABLE MUSCLE.

> BEN: I take after my Dad! He's so strong they call him 'Big
>   Five' because he knocked out five baddies in one go.
>
> ESH: *(Trills loudly)*
>   Passed!
>
> BEN: We're brothers, Man! I mean – mouse!
>
>   THE THREE SLAP HANDS AS 'BROTHERS'.

Cut to
GROUND

LLOYD PRINCE IS STARING UP AT THE SKY WATCHING THE **SAUCER SHAPE** THAT
IS SPINNING HIGHER AND HIGHER. IT ABRUPTLY DISAPPEARS FROM SIGHT.

> LLOYD PRINCE: *(Aloud to himself)*
>   Second time I've seen it. Hope I ain't losing my
>   marbles.

FADE OUT

TAKE 7

It's all down to 'Imagination'

FADE IN

SELESTRA PLATFORM

THE KIDNAPPED CHILDREN, AND TEENAGERS, ARE SITTING TOGETHER ON THE
PLATFORM THAT IS SUSPENDED IN SPACE.

> MARVIN: *(Rubbing his eyes)*
>   This has gotta be a bad dream.
>   *(To Denzil)*
>   Pinch me, Man!

DENZIL OBLIGES.

(Yells)
You sure like pinching!

DENZIL: Now you know you ain't dreaming, Man!

PETE: *(Gloomily)*
We're all having the same nightmare.

TERRY: *(Brightly)*
I know! We're acting in a sci-fi film.

ANDREW: With me playing the lead, I'm training to be an actor.

HE PULLS LANA INTO HIS ARMS.

(Passionately)
My Darlink!

LANA: *(Pushing him away)*
Stop messing about, Andrew, we're in dead trouble.

ANDREW: In trouble, but not *dead* as yet!

JADE: *(Sighing)*
If only I could hear my mum shouting at me like everything's back to normal.

MARVIN LOOKS TOWARDS PIED PIPER WHO IS SITTING CROSS-LEGGED - THE FLUTE RESTING ON HIS KNEES.

MARVIN: Hey, Man, or whatever you are! What is this all about?

PIED PIPER: I'm a Pied Piper and when I play my flute, I get followed - so now you're being taken for a *ride.*

CHILDREN: *(Cry)*
Mum! Mummy! I want to go home.

MARVIN: *(Loudly and cheerfully)*
Kids, did you ever imagine you'd reach the stars?

'THE PETS' LAUNCH INTO A GIG, LED BY MARVIN:

'IMAGINATION' is the stuff of dreams,
So wing away into other realms.
On a magic carpet beyond the stars,
Trip the 'Light Fantastic' on Pluto and Mars.

Then shoot like a falling star below ground,
Where goblins and gremlins abound.
In creepy caverns and caves,
And abysses only you dare brave.

Bring to your arm a magical weapon,
That'll slaughter the monsters that beckon.
Show the world what you're at,
Conjure wondrous tricks from a hat.

Get your thumb into every pie,
Float in a balloon across the sky.
Gas gone! You're falling,
Help! You're calling.

Not to worry!
Don't flurry!
It's only a game,
Called 'IMAGINATION'.

Cut to
A MARROW-SHAPED SHIP

IT LANDS ON THE PLATFORM.

PIED PIPER PUTS HIS FLUTE TO HIS LIPS, HIS FEET JIG AND HE ENTERS THE MARROW SHIP, FOLLOWED BY THE JIGGING CHILDREN.

ON ENTERING THE SHIP, THE CHILDREN ARE GUIDED TO TUB-SHAPE SEATS BY THE THREE MEMBERS OF THE CREW. THE FACE OF EACH ONE IS A GLOSSY WHITE EGG; EYES, NOSE AND MOUTH FINELY ETCHED BLACK OUTLINES. THEIR CLOTHING IS A FULL PANTALOON SUIT THAT HAS A RUFFLE AT THE NECK, WRISTS AND ANKLES AND A RUFFLE TOPPING THE EGG.

GEMMA:	*(Giggles to Kathy)* They're, 'Humpty Dumpties'.
KATHY:	*(Fearfully)* I hope they don't fall down, and spread egg everywhere – Ugh!

THE CREW HAND OUT LOLLIPOPS TO THE CHILDREN.

GEMMA:	*(Noisily sucking)* This lollipop tastes really yummy!
KATHY:	It changes colour with every suck.

Cut to
CONTROLS OF THE SHIP

THEY ARE SITUATED IN THE SAME CABIN AS THE PASSENGERS.

THE **PILOT** IS SITTING AT THE CONTROL PANEL.

SHE IS A STRIKING LOOKING BLACK GIRL. TWO ANTENNAS RISE FROM THE TOP OF HER BRAIDED HAIR THAT IS SPRINKLED WITH STARDUST. LONG THICK CURLING BLACK EYELASHES FRINGE HER SPARKLING BROWN EYES. HER LIPS ARE A GLISTENING ROSY RED AND PARTED SMILINGLY AT THE CHILDREN, REVEALING PEARLY WHITE TEETH. HER SLENDER FIGURE IS CLOTHED IN A WHITE SATIN FLYING SUIT.

MARVIN:	*(To Denzil)* She's a sister, Man!
PILOT:	*(Speaking into an instrument in her hand)* Welcome aboard! We are on course to Planet Moona. My crew and I wish you *Boomps a Daisy* and thank you for flying *Moon Madness*.

Cut to
THE GALAXY

THE SHIP IS FLYING SERENELY ACROSS THE GALAXY LEAVING BEHIND A MISTY TRAIL THAT **PICKS UP STARS** AND CARRIES THEM ALONG WITH IT.

Cut to

MOON ROLLOVER

IT IS SHIMMERED OVER BY THE LIGHT OF A BROAD SILVER MOON.

THE MARROW SHIP LANDS.

PIED PIPER, PLAYING HIS FLUTE AND JIGGING, FOLLOWED BY THE JIGGING CHILDREN, ENTER THE 'MOON ROLLOVER'.

THE STARS THAT WERE CAUGHT IN THE MARROW SHIP'S MISTY TRAIL FOLLOW THE CHILDREN INSIDE.

HUMP WOBBLES WITH PLEASURE AT THE SIGHT OF THE CHILDREN.

HUMP:	The children look a healthy lot, Pied Piper.
PIED PIPER:	Have you got the Golden Fleece for me, Hump?
HUMP:	You'll have it, Pied Piper, not to worry! I've got Trunka the tinker onto it and you can place a winning bet he'll find a way of filching it from the Red Dragon.
	HE CALLS TO THE CHILDREN OF HAMELIN.
	Come over here children of Hamelin!
	THE CHILDREN LISTLESSLY WANDER OVER.
	Show this new lot how to *spit and polish*.
KATHY:	(Wagging her finger at Hump, her voice prim) It's rude to spit.
HUMP:	(Snaps at her) Polish, then!

Cut to

FUN MACHINES

THE TEENAGERS ARE WATCHING THE STARS THAT CAME INTO THE MOON ROLLOVER, PLAYING ON THE MACHINES. WHENEVER A STAR LOSES, IT THROWS UP A CLOUD OF DUST.

ANDREW:	So much for, 'stars in your eyes'.

THE GROUP GIG, LED BY MARVIN:

'Here on planet Moona,
All the stars are loona!
Gambling the night away,
The Galaxy's in disarray.

Twinkle, twinkle, little star,
How I wonder where you are?
No diamond shining in the sky,
Up above our world so high.

No more guiding light
Glistening in the night.
No more 'Wishing on a star',
From our world afar.

We'll be back one day,
Travelling the 'Milky Way'.
Twinkle, twinkle, how time flies,
When STARS GET IN YOUR EYES.'

FADE OUT

TAKE 8

The MOONMIFS

FADE IN

A PLATFORM IN SPACE

ESH'S SHIP HAS LANDED.

ON THE PLATFORM IS AN ENORMOUS PUMP. ESH DEPRESSES A CONTROL AND A LIGHT FLASHES SIMULTANEOUSLY WITH THE LIGHTS ENCIRCLING THE SHIP. THERE IS A LOUD GURGLING NOISE.

Cut to

FLOCK OF BIRDS

THEY ARE FLYING TOWARDS THE PLATFORM CARRYING A BIRD OF THE FLOCK BETWEEN THEM.

THERE IS A BIG RUSH OF WINGS AS THEY LAND ON THE PLATFORM.

THE BIRDS ARE GREY SCRAGGY-LOOKING CREATURES, WITH LONG SHARP RED BEAKS.

ONE OF THE BIRDS HOPS UP TO ESH.

MOOKIN:	I am Mookin, the leader of the Moonmifs. My wife Mookina has injured her wing and cannot fly. Only the healing rays of planet Wizlaxia can mend it. - Without the use of her wing Mookina will surely die.
ESH:	I'm flying to Wizlaxia. - I'd be happy to take your wife along in my ship.
MOOKIN:	Bless you, Mouse! I shall never forget your kindness.
BEN:	*(To Mookina)* I'll carry you to the ship.
MOOKINA:	*(Mews sweetly)* Thank you my dear. I'm able to hop.

ESH, THE BOYS, AND MOOKINA HOPPING ALONG, BOARD THE SHIP.

IT FLIES ONWARDS.

BEN:	How did your wing get broken, Mookina?
MOOKINA:	It was struck by a rock thrown up by the Moonseas during a storm. *(Sighs)* It's a hard life living on the Moonseas.
JAMES:	Can't you live somewhere else?
MOOKINA:	*(Sadly)* Living on the Moonseas is our punishment.
BEN:	*(Incredulous)* Punishment?
MOOKINA:	Would you like to hear the sad story of the Moonmifs?
BEN:	If you can bear to tell us?
MOOKINA:	*Long, long ago, the Moonmifs were beautiful WHITE DOVES and for many Millenniums they flew together in perfect love and harmony.*

FLASHBACK:
FLYING ACROSS A SERENE BLUE SKY ARE BEAUTIFUL SILVERY WHITE DOVES.

MOOKINA:	*There came a time when the doves wished to go their separate ways and the love and harmony that had existed between them turned into envy and greed and fighting with one another.*

FLASHBACK:
THE DOVES ARE FIGHTING AND PECKING ONE ANOTHER – FEATHERS FLY.

MOOKINA:	*As a punishment, the Kindred Spirit changed the doves into the drab birds we are now, destined to dwell forever on the harsh Moonseas.*

Cut to
MOONSEAS
IT IS A STARK SCENE OF CRAGGY PEAKS AND A STONY GROUND.

JAMES:	*(Solemnly)* Your story has a moral to it, Mookina.

FADE OUT

TAKE 9

Four legged COWBOYS

FADE IN

TANGLER LAND

STABLES ARE DOTTED ABOUT ON A REDDISH EARTHY TERRAIN.

ESH'S SPACESHIP COMES INTO SIGHT FLYING ACROSS A CLEAR BLUE SKY.

THE DOORS TO THE STABLES BURST OPEN AND GALLOPING OUT OF THEM ARE **HORSES.** THEY WEAR THE CLOTHING OF COWBOYS. ON THEIR HEAD SITS A LARGE SOMBRERO; THE OUTFIT COMPLETED BY A LEATHER WAISTCOAT AND TROUSERS INDENTED WITH GLEAMING STUDS.

THEY NEIGH LOUDLY AND GALLOP IN LEAPS THAT CARRY THEM HIGH ABOVE THE GROUND. THEY ARE TWIRLING LASSOES SKY HIGH.

THE LASSOES ENCIRCLE THE SHIP AND IT IS PULLED DOWN TO THE GROUND.

NED, THE LEADER OF THE TANGLERS, AND LARGER THAN THE OTHERS, KICKS THE SHIP WITH HIS HOOF.

TANGLER NED:	*(Neighing loudly)* Open up, or we'll spin you around so fast you won't know whether you're coming or going!
	ESH AND THE BOYS APPEAR STANDING OUTSIDE THE SHIP.
	Where are you flying to mouse?
ESH:	Wizlaxia - the planet of the rainbow.
TANGLER NED:	*(Neighs excitedly to the others)* That's where the crock of gold is, fellers! We'll take the mouse along with us to help us nab it!
ESH:	*(Trills horrified)* The crock of gold is kept in the maze at the foot of the rainbow and only the Sorcerer knows the path leading to it. Why do you want to steal the crock?

TANGLER NED: All that lovely *lolly* to gamble on the fun machines in the 'Moon Rollover'.
(To the other Tanglers)
Tie up the mouse.
(Hee-hawing laughter)
And those two funnies!

BEN: *(Scowling)*
Funny yourself, Man! I mean *horse*!

ESH AND THE BOYS, LASSOES AROUND THEM, ARE PULLED AWAY FROM THE SHIP.

WHOOPING AND NEIGHING, THE TANGLERS LASSO TREES LADEN WITH APPLES AND SHAKE THE BRANCHES BRISKLY SO THAT THE FRUIT FALLS TO THE GROUND.

THEY PELT THE PRISONERS WITH THE APPLES AND THE THREE WRIGGLE ABOUT HELPLESSLY TRYING TO AVOID BEING HIT BY THE FRUIT.

TIRING OF THE SPORT, THE TANGLERS GALLOP OFF TOWARDS A RANGE OF LOW MOUNTAINS AND DISAPPEAR BEYOND THEM.

FADE OUT

TAKE 10

RED DRAGON gets fleeced

FADE IN

LAND OF COLCHIS

TRUNKA THE TINKER IS DRIVING HIS CART. HE IS SHORT IN STATURE AND HAS THE HEAD AND TRUNK OF AN ELEPHANT.

TRUNKA: *(Sings)*
Any old jumble, bits and pieces,
Black Holes, meteorites, quasars, rocks,
Extra Terrestrials, Flying Saucers,
Trunka the tinker buys the crocks.

HE SIGHTS THE **RED DRAGON**, SWIRLING FLAMES. HE GETS OUT OF THE CART
AND PLODS UP TO WITHIN A SAFE DISTANCE OF THE FLAMES.

TRUNKA:	*(Snorts loudly)* Hi, Red Dragon! Still blowing your top?
RED DRAGON:	*(Bad tempered rasping voice)* Don't you know I'm guarding the Golden Fleece?
TRUNKA:	I've brought you an invitation from Hump, the ruler of Planet Moona, to his 'Moon Rollover' Turnover. TRUNKA HOLDS UP THE INVITATION THEN LAYS IT ON THE GROUND. RED DRAGON RETRIEVES IT WITH A LONG ARM.
RED DRAGON:	Hump writes, 'He's inviting me because I'm real hot stuff'. I've never been to a party *(Sorrowfully)* I've never ever been beyond Colchis.
TRUNKA:	So, now's your chance.
RED DRAGON:	I've nothing to wear for a party except the Golden Fleece and that's too small for me.

THIS IS THE LEAD TRUNKA HAS BEEN WAITING FOR.

TRUNKA:	I'll do a deal with you, Red Dragon! You give me that old fleece, it'll keep me warm when I'm travelling the 'Ice Bounds', and I'll give you in exchange the mantle of Mandarin Choo Choo of China. - I'll show it to you. HE RUNS TO HIS CART AND REMOVES THE MANTLE FROM IT. HE HOLDS THE MANTLE UP FOR RED DRAGON TO SEE. IT IS RED SILK, EMROIDERED IN GOLD THREADS THAT GLEAM LIKE FIRE IN THE SUNLIGHT. Imagine yourself wearing it, Red Dragon. You'll look magnificent!

RED DRAGON:	Oooh! It's gorgeous. *(Suspiciously)* What are you doing with the Mandarin's mantle?
TRUNKA:	Mandarin Choo Choo gave it to me as a reward for saving his life when he landed on the wrong side of the Great Wall of China during a battle. My trunk hoisted him back to his side of it.
RED DRAGON:	*(Swirling his head about)* But I'm bound by mythology to guard the Golden Fleece.
TRUNKA:	You're Millenniums behind the times! You've got to concern yourself with the *here and now*.
RED DRAGON:	*(Obstinately)* I've *got* to have something to guard and the only thing as precious as the Golden Fleece is the crock of gold at the end of the rainbow.
TRUNKA:	Nah! There's nothing in the crock, it's all a myth.
RED DRAGON:	I don't believe you!
TRUNKA:	Trust me! I get around and I know everything that's going on in the galaxy. If you must guard something precious, then guard my **clobber.** It's so precious that if it was to get stolen, the galaxy would be in deep deep trouble.
RED DRAGON:	I've never heard of clobber. Show it to me.

TRUNKA PULLS A SACK FROM HIS CART AND DRAGS IT ALONG THE GROUND UNTIL IT IS FACING THE RED DRAGON

TRUNKA:	My *clobber* is in this sack. *(Waving his trunk)* Come to think of it, my clobber is too precious - even for a brave dragon like you to guard.
	HE BEGINS TO DRAG THE SACK BACK TOWARDS THE CART.

RED DRAGON: *(Rasping loudly)*
                   Oooh! I must guard your clobber! Please! Please!

TRUNKA: *(Waving his trunk)*
                   Calm down or you'll burn yourself out! I'll let you guard
                   my clobber, but don't you go looking inside the sack.
                   The shock of seeing my precious clobber could put your
                   flames out forever.

RED DRAGON: Oooh! I'm proud to be trusted with your precious
                   clobber.

TRUNKA: I'm proud to have such a brave dragon as a friend. –
                   Mind if I fill a can with your spit-outs? My cart is low on
                   fuel.

RED DRAGON: Go ahead! It's so lovely to have a friend.

TRUNKA: 'Giving' is what friendship is all about.
                   (Voice only audible to himself)
                   'A friend in need – is a friend indeed.'

TRUNKA QUICKLY PULLS THE GOLDEN FLEECE OFF THE BRANCH OF A TREE WHERE
IT IS HANGING. HE RACES WITH THE FLEECE AS FAST AS HIS LEGS WILL CARRY
HIM TO HIS CART, FEARING RED DRAGON MIGHT CHANGE HIS MIND.

TRUNKA: *(Waving his trunk at the dragon)*
                   Bye friend! See you in the 'Moon Rollover'.

                   HE DRIVES HIS CART SWIFTLY AWAY.

FADE OUT

TAKE 11

MOONMIFS to the rescue

FADE IN

TANGLER LAND

A LIT UP PATH EXTENDS FROM THE SPACESHIP AND **MOOKINA** IS SLOWLY HOPPING ALONG IT.

SHE HOPS TOWARDS ESH AND THE BOYS WHO ARE SITTING ON THE GROUND – A LASSO AROUND EACH ONE.

WITH HER LONG SHARP BEAK, SHE PECKS AT THE LASSO AROUND **ESH.** IT IS BITTEN THROUGH AND THE MOUSE RACES MADLY TOWARDS THE SHIP.

MOOKINA THEN PECKS AT THE LASSO AROUND JAMES, FREEING HIM. HE RACES AFTER ESH.

MOOKINA BEGINS PECKING AT THE LASSO AROUND BEN.

THE TANGLERS ARE RETURNING.

HOOVES THUNDER, LASSOES WHIRL AND THE NEIGHING OF THE TANGLERS FILL THE AIR.

A TANGLER WHIRLS A LASSO OVER MOOKINA AND BEN. IT IS PULLED SO TIGHTLY THE BIRD IS SQUEEZED AGAINST BEN'S CHEST.

A LOUD MEWING COMES FROM MOOKINA'S THROAT THAT EERILY REVERBERATES.

THE TANGLER RAISES A HOOF ABOVE MOOKINA AND BEN, PREPARING TO STAMP THEM TO DEATH.

MOONMIFS COME INTO VIEW FLYING OVERHEAD.

THE TANGLERS MADLY WHIRL THEIR LASSOES, BUT THE MOONMIFS SKILFULLY FLY OUT OF THEIR REACH.

MOOKIN FLIES TO WHERE THE TANGLER HAS HIS HOOF RAISED ABOVE MOOKINA AND BEN. HE PLUNGES HIS BEAK INTO THE TANGLER'S EYE. OTHER MOONMIFS PECK THE TANGLER'S RUMP. IT JUMPS AND NEIGHS IN AGONY.

THE LASSO AROUND BEN AND MOOKINA IS BITTEN THROUGH.

HOLDING MOOKINA UNDER HIS ARM, BEN RACES TOWARDS THE SHIP.

THERE IS A MAD FORAY OF MOONMIFS' BEAKS AND THE WHIRLING OF LASSOES AROUND THE SHIP.

BEN REACHES THE SHIP AND THE LIGHTED PATH DRAWS HIM AND MOOKINA SAFELY INTO IT.

THE SHIP RISES INTO THE AIR AND VERY SOON LEAVES THE TANGLERS BEHIND.

FADE OUT

TAKE 12

A cat and mouse game

FADE IN

LAND OF COLCHIS

THE SPACESHIP IS FLYING ACROSS A CLEAR BLUE SKY. IT BEGINS TO SHUDDER VIOLENTLY.

Cut to
INT: SHIP

ESH IS AT THE CONTROLS DESPERATELY TRYING TO RIGHT THE SHIP.

ESH:	I'm short on fuel and the next platform is a long way off. I'll have to make a forced landing in the city below.
MOOKINA:	*(Mews terrified)* It's a land of cats, ruled over by the wicked cat Queen Medea.
ESH:	Cats! That's bad news for a mouse!

THE SPACESHIP SAFELY LANDS.

ESH AND THE BOYS ALIGHT FROM THE SHIP.

THERE IS A LOUD TINKLING OF BELLS.

THERE COMES INTO VIEW **QUEEN MEDEA**, A GLAMOROUS JET BLACK CAT, WEARING A GOLDEN CROWN AND RECLINING ON A LUXURIOUS VELVET COUCH THAT IS BORNE ALONG BY HER SOLDIERS.

FOLLOWING BEHIND THE COUCH IS A PROCESSION OF CATS, ALL SIZES AND COLOURS, PADDING UPRIGHT ON THEIR BACK PAWS. AROUND THE NECK OF EACH CAT IS A GOLD COLLAR WITH A BELL.

| ESH: | *(Worriedly)*
This is going to be a real *cat and mouse* game. |

QUEEN MEDEA POINTS A JEWELLED PAW AT ESH.

MEDEA:	Cook that mouse for tonight's banquet.
ESH:	You'll have tummy ache. I'm on antibiotics.
MEDEA:	*(Spits)* *On*e of my spells will deal with that. - Onwards to my palace, bearers!

ESH AND THE BOYS ARE HURRIED ROUGHLY ALONG BETWEEN MEDIA'S SOLDIERS.

Cut to
PALACE

IT IS A MAGNIFICENT GRECIAN STRUCTURE COMPLETE WITH MARBLE COLUMNS. MASSIVE CLAY POTS ARE DOTTED ALL AROUND. THEY CONTAIN EXOTIC PLANTS THAT WAVE EERILY ABOUT. ALL ALONG THE LEAVES OF THE PLANTS ARE ROUND STARING EYES.

THE COUCH BEARING QUEEN MEDEA IS CARRIED INTO THE PALACE AND IS BORNE PAST A PARAKEET CHAINED TO A POST.

| PARAKEET: | *(Squarks)*
Queen Medea - the fairest in the land. |
| MEDEA: | *(Purrs)*
My, Para! Para! |

ESH IS HUSTLED OUT OF SIGHT BY THE SOLDIERS.

| MEDEA: | *(To the boys)*
You Earthlings may attend my banquet. |

Cut to

BANQUETING HALL

QUEEN MEDEA SITS ON A THRONE AT THE HEAD OF THE BANQUETING TABLE. THE BOYS SIT EITHER SIDE OF HER.

THE QUEEN DIPS HER PAW INTO A BOWL OF SWIMMING GOLDFISH, AND STUFFS THEM GREEDILY INTO HER MOUTH. SHE THEN DROPS A GOLDFISH ONTO BEN'S PLATE.

MEDEA: *(Commands)*
Eat up!

BEN WRINKLES HIS NOSE IN DISGUST AT THE WRIGGLING GOLDFISH.

BEN: I'm allergic to fish, Your Majesty! I come out in a rash!

ONE OF THE SERVANTS IS POURING MILK FROM A JUG INTO A LARGE GOLDEN SAUCER AND PLACES IT BEFORE THE QUEEN.

MEDEA: Give the Earthlings a saucer of milk.

THE SERVANT POURS MILK INTO SAUCERS, PLACING THEM IN FRONT OF THE BOYS.

MEDEA GREEDILY LAPS THE MILK IN HER SAUCER, STOPS AND GLARES AT JAMES.

MEDEA: *(To James)*
Lap up!

JAMES BENDS HIS HEAD AND TRIES TO IMITATE THE QUEEN'S LAPPING.

(Screeches at James)
Your tongue's a vile colour.

SERVANTS CARRY TO THE TABLE A LARGE SILVER TUREEN.

MEDEA: *(Purring loudly)*
'MOUSEE FRICASEE'.

BEN: *(Covers his eyes with his hands)*
I can't bear to look!

THE LID OF THE TUREEN IS LIFTED.

ESH IS SITTING UPRIGHT ON THE DISH, GARNISHES ALL OVER HIM.

| ESH: | (Trills grinning)
No cookie, Medea! I'm a Whizmouse! I hacked into the microwave. |

ESH JUMPS OFF THE DISH AND SWIFTLY SCAMPERS TOWARDS THE EXIT OF THE PALACE.

THE BOYS JUMP UP AND RACE AFTER ESH.

| MEDEA: | (Shrieks)
After them! |

THE SOLDIERS GIVE CHASE AND THE THREE ARE CAPTURED.

| MEDEA: | (Spitting at them)
No-one escapes Queen Medea. I'll change you into plants and you'll be forever rooted in pots along with the others who tried to cross me.
(To her soldiers)
Lock them up in a dungeon. |

Cut to
DUNGEON

ESH AND THE BOYS ARE PUSHED ROUGHLY INSIDE AND JOIN TWO PRISONERS.
A BOY AND GIRL.

| BEN: | (Wide eyed)
You're the boy and girl from the Hamelin clock in Mr Popov's shop? |

| BOY: | Yes! We're brother and sister. – My name is Tristan. |

| GIRL: | My name is Isolda. |

| JAMES: | (To Tristan)
Your eye did blink? |

| TRISTAN: | (Nods)
The light from your torch. |

| JAMES: | Sorry! |

| BEN: | So how did you two get here? |

TRISTAN: It's a long story, but I'll make it short! – One day a Pied Piper came to Hamelin and fluted away all the children, except us - that's because our father the keeper of the clock tower kept his back to the door to prevent us leaving, although our feet were jigging madly.

JAMES: *(Sharply)*
I know that story! The Citizens of Hamelin refused to pay the Pied Piper the promised reward for ridding the city of the rats, so he took his revenge.

ISOLDA: *(Sadly)*
It wasn't the citizens' fault. The greedy Mayor of Hamelin wanted to keep the reward for himself.

TRISTAN: *(Miserably)*
I'm hungry.

BEN OFFERS A BISCUIT FROM HIS POCKET.

TRISTAN BITES INTO THE BISCUIT AND VERY SLOWLY CRUNCHES IT BETWEEN HIS TEETH.

THE BOYS WRIGGLE IMPATIENTLY – ON TENDERHOOKS TO HEAR THE REST OF THE STORY.

JAMES FINALLY LETS OUT A LOUD SIGH, HINTING TO TRISTAN TO CONTINUE.

TRISTAN: *(Frowning)*
I remember my Mama saying, 'I was to chew my food properly, twenty-six times at least'.

ISOLDA: *(Takes up the story)*
One day, Old Father Time came to Hamelin –

FLASHBACK:
CLOCK TOWER - CITY OF HAMELIN

OLD FATHER TIME, HAVING LONG FLOWING WHITE HAIR AND A FLOWING WHITE BEARD, STOPS AT THE CLOCK TOWER. STANDING WITHIN ITS PORTALS ARE TRISTAN AND ISOLDA.

OLD FATHER TIME: Why are there no other children in this city except for yourselves and a lame boy?

ISOLDA:	(Sadly) All the other children were fluted away by a Pied Piper. No-one knows where he's taken them and they've never been seen since.
OLD FATHER TIME:	That's very sad. HE DANGLES THE OLD POCKET WATCH. This watch has stopped ticking. I shall send you with the watch to someone who can get it ticking again. When that happens, you will find yourselves in the palace of the witch, Queen Medea. There you must seek out the 'Centuries Timetable' she stole from me. In it is written the time the hands of the watch should be turned to, so that the time in Hamelin returns to what it was before the Pied Piper came to the city.

BACK TO THE DUNGEON:

ISOLDA:	When Mr Popov got the watch ticking again, we found ourselves in this palace and Queen Medea threw us into this dungeon.
TRISTAN:	(Miserably) Really threw us - we're bruised all over.
ISOLDA:	(Tearfully) And whatever happened to the pocket watch?
BEN:	(Loud cheerful voice) Here it is! DANGLES THE POCKET WATCH BY ITS CHAIN.

FADE OUT

TAKE 13

A big change

FADE IN

CAT LAND

TRUNKA COMES INTO VIEW DRIVING HIS CART.

HE SEES THE PARKED SPACESHIP, GETS OUT OF THE CART AND GOES UP TO IT.

TRUNKA:	Hello! Anyone about?

MOOKINA APPEARS HOPPING SLOWLY DOWN THE SHINY PATH THAT EXTENDS FROM THE SHIP.

MOOKINA:	The pilot of this ship has been taken away by Queen Medea. *(Mews sadly)* She's probably eaten him up by now – him being a mouse.
TRUNKA:	The mouse wouldn't happen to be my pal, 'Ever So Helpful' ESH?
MOOKINA:	Yes!
TRUNKA:	He should know better than to land in a country of cats.
MOOKINA:	The ship ran out of fuel, he had to make a forced landing.
TRUNKA:	Any passengers?
MOOKINA:	Two children from Planet Earth. SHE HOPS UP TO TRUNKA'S CART. I see you've got the Golden Fleece?
TRUNKA:	Yeah! I did a deal with the Red Dragon.
MOOKINA:	Did you know that whoever puts on the Golden Fleece has the power to change into the likeness of somebody else?

TRUNKA:	*(Snorting to himself)* That could come in handy.
MOOKINA:	*(Mewing excitedly)* If you were to change yourself into the likeness of Prince Jason, the queen would do anything for you. It's hot gossip that she's still so madly in love with the prince she never stops cat-a-wailing for his return.
TRUNKA:	*(Waving his trunk)* Nah! It's too risky! How can I be sure I'll change back into myself again? If I don't, my Missus will blow her trunk, I can tell you!
MOOKINA:	Please give it a try Trunka. ESH may still be alive.
TRUNKA:	Well, if there's a chance to save my pal!
	HE REMOVES THE FLEECE FROM THE CART AND LAYS IT OUT ON THE GROUND.
	THE HEAD OF THE RAM IS ATTACHED TO THE FLEECE.
RAM:	Baaah! Baaah! - Say, *'Quickchange me'* into whoever you want to be.
TRUNKA:	*(Astounded)* You can talk!
RAM:	Baaah! Baaah! I've nearly forgotten how. I've been asleep for Millenniums. - There's a *quickchange* limit of forty tickovers.
TRUNKA:	How long is 'forty tickovers'?
RAM:	I can't remember! Imagine yourself counting sheep. I never get to forty - I'm snoozing before then.
MOOKINA:	Please give it a try, Trunka. Only you can carry it off – you've got the 'gift of the gab'.

TRUNKA DRAPES THE FLEECE ACROSS HIS SHOULDERS.

FADE OUT

TAKE 14

Enter Prince Jason

FADE IN

QUEEN MEDEA'S PALACE

A HANDSOME CAT ENTERS.

MEDEA LOOKS AT HIM IN AMAZEMENT.

MEDEA: *(Screeches)*
          Jason! My beloved Prince!

TRUNKA: *(Purrs)*
          Medea! My unforgettable Pussykins. I've returned to
          hold you once again to my furry breast.

MEDEA: *(Cat-a-wails)*
          Where have you been this last millennium?

TRUNKA: It's a long story.
          (Softly to himself)
          I'm still working on it!
          Let's not waste time on the past my love – here and
          now is what matters!
          (Worriedly under his breath)
          Time is ticking by!
          (Placing his arms around Medea's waist)
          To your bedchamber my sweet Pussykins!

          TRUNKA'S ARM IS AROUND MEDEA'S WAIST AS SHE
          LEADS HIM TOWARDS HER BED CHAMBER.

          ALONG THE WAY THEY PASS THE PARAKEET.

PARAKEET: *(Squarks)*
          Trunka tinker!

MEDEA TRIES TO COME TO A HALT, BUT TRUNKA URGENTLY PROPELS HER
FORWARD, WHISPERING IN HER EAR.

MEDEA: *(Purring ecstatically, her golden eyes rolling)*
          Oh, Jason, How I adore your 'Sweet Nothings'.

Cut to

BEDCHAMBER

TRUNKA TAKES MEDEA INTO HIS ARMS, THEN DRAWS BACK, FINGERING A LARGE
GOLDEN KEY HANGING ON A NECKLACE AROUND MEDEA'S NECK.

TRUNKA: Take off your necklace, My Beloved. The key digs into
my breast.

MEDEA: I cannot do that, my Prince.
(Fingering the key)
This is the key to my Kingdom - my most precious
possession.

TRUNKA: More precious than your Prince Jason?

MEDEA: *(Wavering voice)*
No o o!

TRUNKA: Then take off the necklace and put it in the urn by your
bedside - it'll be safe there.

MEDEA MUTELY SHAKES HER HEAD.

Then I shall kiss your sweet paws and be gone.

MEDEA: *(Cat-a-wails)*
No! No! Jason! You must never leave me again.

SHE QUICKLY TAKES OFF THE NECKLACE AND DROPS
IT INTO THE URN.

TRUNKA: Now recline on your couch, my beloved, close your
eyes and await your Prince Jason's kiss - as though you
are the 'Sleeping Beauty'.

MEDEA: *(Purring loudly)*
Ooh, Jason! You're so romantic.

MEDEA RECLINES ON THE FOUR-POSTER BED, HER
EYES CLOSED.

TRUNKA QUICKLY DIPS INTO THE URN, REMOVES THE NECKLACE AND TIPTOES
OUT OF THE CHAMBER.

TRUNKA: *(Fingering the key)*
Now where can ESH be?

Cut to
DUNGEON

TRUNKA FINDS HIMSELF STANDING IN FRONT OF THE DUNGEON – IN IT ARE ESH AND THE OTHERS.

| TRUNKA: | *(To the guards)*
Release the prisoners! |

SEEING A CAT THE IMAGE OF PRINCE JASON, THE GUARDS OBEY.

| TRUNKA: | *(Sternly to the prisoners)*
Move! |

                              TRUNKA, ESH AND THE CHILDREN RACE ALONG.

| TRUNKA: | *(Very quietly)*
Hi, ESH! It's me, Trunka! |

| ESH: | *(Trilling loudly in shock)*
Trunka! How come you're a Prince Tomcat? |

| TRUNKA: | Shhh! No time to explain; any tickover I could change back into my own self. |

AS THEY PASS THE PARAKEET IT SQUARKS.

| PARAKEET: | Trunka tinker! |

THE SOLDIER ON DUTY LOOKS SUSPICIOUSLY IN TRUNKA'S DIRECTION.

TRUNKA REMOVES THE CLOAK HE IS WEARING AND FLINGS IT OVER THE CAGE COMPLETELY CONCEALING IT.

| TRUNKA: | Sleepy Byes. |

THEY EXIT FROM THE PALACE.

Cut to
SPOOKY LEANING TOWER

SMOKE IS CURLING FROM THE CHIMNEY OF THE TOWER.

| ISOLDA: | It's Medea's Coven, where the *'Centuries timetable'* is kept. |

THEY ENTER THE COVEN.

IN THE COVEN ARE LOTS OF GRUESOME-LOOKING OBJECTS, HUMAN AND ANIMAL SKULLS, AND CONTAINERS FILLED WITH COLOURED LIQUID.

TRISTAN AND ISOLDA, SEARCH FRANTICALLY AMONGST A PILE OF BOOKS.

BEN PICKS UP A POUCH AND LOOKS INSIDE IT.

BEN: Seeds! I'll take them for Mookina, she must be hungry by now.

TRISTAN: (Holding up a book yellowed with age)
                I've found the 'Centuries Timetable'.

THEY QUICKLY LEAVE THE COVEN.

FADE OUT

TAKE 15

Prince Uncharming

FADE IN

MEDEA'S BEDCHAMBER

MEDEA IS BECOMING IMPATIENT. SHE RAISES HER HEAD, HER EYES STILL CLOSED.

MEDEA: (Purring loudly)
                My Prince, I can't wait a hundred years like the Sleeping Beauty. Kiss me, now, this very minute.

                SHE PLOPS HER HEAD BACK ON THE PILLOW EXPECTANTLY. A FEW SECONDS ELAPSE, SHE OPENS ONE EYE, THEN THE OTHER, THEN SITS BOLT UPRIGHT AND LOOKS AROUND THE ROOM.

                (Cat-a-wailing)
                Where are you Jason?

                HER FACE GRIMACES AS THE TRUTH BEGINS TO DAWN.

SHE DIPS INTO THE URN, HER EYES GOGGLE.

(Shrieks)
The key's gone!

SHE PICKS UP A HAND MIRROR AND LOOKS INTO IT.
TRUNKA HAS CHANGED BACK INTO HIS OWN SELF.

(Cat-a-wails)
The cheating elephant!

SHE JUMPS UP FROM THE BED, RUSHES TO THE DOOR
OF THE CHAMBER, OPENS IT AND SHRIEKS

Guards! Guards!

Cut to
OUTSIDE PALACE

TRUNKA AND THE OTHERS ARE HURRYING TOWARDS HIS CART.

A LARGE FORCE OF SOLDIERS HEADED BY MEDEA, BORNE ALONG ON THE COUCH,
ARE APPROACHING.

MEDEA:	*(Spitting and cat-a-wailing)* Claw them to death! – Claw them to death!

TRUNKA QUICKLY REMOVES MEDEA'S NECKLACE FROM A POCKET IN HIS
DUNGAREES AND WHIRLS IT BY ITS KEY ABOVE HIS HEAD.

TRUNKA:	*(Loudly)* GET LOST!

THE SOLDIERS, MEDEA AND HER PALACE VANISH INTO THIN AIR.

Cut to
SPACESHIP

ESH:	*(Sadly to Trunka)* I can't fly my ship - I've run out of fuel.
TRUNKA:	How far do you want to go?
ESH:	Wizlaxia – the planet of the rainbow.

TRUNKA:	I can help you out!
	HE REMOVES A CAN FROM HIS CART.
	The Red Dragon's spit-outs - there's enough in the can to fly your ship to Wizlaxia.
ESH:	Trunka! You're the best friend a mouse ever had!
TRUNKA:	Well, one favour deserves another! Remember how you helped me when a gangster after my ivory tusks flung a net over me? And do you remember what I said?
ESH:	(Trills, grinning) 'How can a wee mouse help an elephant?'
TRUNKA:	Right! You gnawed a hole in the net and saved my life.

ESH AND THE CHILDREN BOARD THE SHIP.

| MOOKINA: | (Mews sweetly to the boys) Glad to see you again, my dears. |

BEN GIVES MOOKINA THE POUCH OF SEEDS AND SHE LIGHTLY PECKS HIS CHEEK WITH HER BEAK AS A KISS.

THE SHIP LIFTS OFF.

FADE OUT

TAKE 16

Over the rainbow

FADE IN

THE GALAXY

THE SPACESHIP IS FLYING ALONG.

THE ANIMALS REPRESENTING THE STAR CONSTELLATIONS WAVE TO THE SHIP.

THE **'GREAT BEAR'** AND THE **'LITTLE BEAR'** ON THE CONSTELLATIONS: 'URSA MAJOR' AND 'URSA MINOR'.

THE **'BIG DOG'**, AND THE **'LITTLE DOG'**, ON THE CONSTELLATIONS: 'CANIS MAJOR' AND 'CANIS MINOR'.

A **BULL** COMES INTO VIEW.

BEN:	I know the name of that constellation! It's Taurus, my birth-sign.

THE **RAM** COMES INTO SIGHT.

JAMES:	That's Aries, *my* birth-sign.
ESH:	*(Trills)* We're approaching Wizlaxia.

Cut to
A RAINBOW

THE SKY IS ABLAZE WITH A DAZZLING, MASSIVE, SPECTACULAR RAINBOW THAT DOMINATES ALL WITHIN ITS ARC.

THE SHIP LANDS.

MOOKINA:	Goodbye, my dears.
	SHE HOPS OFF, THE BAG OF SEEDS HANGING FROM HER BEAK.

Cut to
THE MAZE

IT IS A ZIGZAG STRUCTURE.

RACING FRANTICALLY AROUND IN CIRCLES IN FRONT OF THE MAZE IS A **HARE**.

ESH:	Hi! Hare! What are you doing away from your Constellation Lepus?
HARE:	The Tanglers lassoed me off it to hare-out the crock of gold in the maze. Don't know how I'll ever get back home.
ESH:	Not to worry Hare! I'll fly you back to it in my ship. *(To the children)* Wait here. I must go inside the maze for a short while and pay my respects to the sorcerer.

Cut to
THE SORCERER

HE IS GAZING DOWN AT ESH FROM HIS GREAT HEIGHT.

SORCERER:	*(Roars)* The crock of gold has gone!
ESH:	The Tanglers stole it to gamble the gold in the 'Moon Rollover' on planet Moona.

THE SORCERER HANDS ESH A ROLLED UP PARCHMENT.

SORCERER:	Your next lot of jobs.
	ESH BOWS LOW TO THE SORCERER.

FADE OUT

TAKE 17

Horoscopes galore

FADE IN

MOON ROLLOVER

HUMP IS SITTING BESIDE **QUEEN DENDERRA.** SHE IS WEARING A WHITE SATIN GOWN EMBROIDERED WITH FLASHING CRYSTALS. AROUND HER NECK ARE NECKLACES OF CRYSTALS. HER LUXURIOUS DARK HAIR IS PILED HIGH INTO A COCKSCOMB STUDDED WITH CRYSTALS. SHE HAS BIG ROUND DARK-EYES; HER LIPS ARE FULL AND ROSY-RED.

CANDIOLLA, A YOUNG SLENDER GOLDEN-HAIRED BEAUTY, ENTERS THE CHAMBER. SHE IS SIGHING DEEPLY.

QUEEN DENDERRA:	Who are you in love with, now, Candiolla?
CANDIOLLA:	God Anchises. *(Drools)* He's so handsome.
QUEEN DENDERRA:	Looks aren't everything, Candiolla! They can deceive. Anchises is a flirt, he just lifts his little finger and all the stars come running.
HUMP:	If you wish to know who your true love is, have your horoscope cast. I've invited all the star signs.
CANDIOLLA:	I'll do that.

Cut to
HOROSCOPE STAR SIGNS

THE TEENAGERS ARRIVE ON THE SCENE AND LAUNCH INTO A GIG:

MARVIN IS THE LEAD SINGER:

> *'Roll up! Roll up! Horoscopes galore!*
> *Astrology predicts what's in store.*
> *Happy, sad, or a disastrous spell,*
> *It's down to what the stars foretell!*

If you're AQUARIUS the water carrier,
Thirst will never be a barrier.

If you're PISCES the fish,
With chips you'll be a favourite dish!

If you're ARIES the ram,
Your antlers will get you out of a jam.

If you're TAURUS the bull,
Your life will never standstill.

If you're a GEMINI twin,
You're in for a double win.

If you're CANCER you'll never roam
Far away from 'home-sweet-home'.

If you're LEO the lion, your roar,
Will scare off those you deplore!

If you're VIRGO, you're the innocent kind,
'Pure and simple' fills your mind.

If you're LIBRA, your claws hide,
Your soft and tender side.

If you're SCORPIO you've got a sting,
That'll make your enemies zing!

If you're SAGITTARIUS, your arrows will fly,
Straight to the heart of the winning bullseye.

If you're CAPRICORN, striving for fame,
Is the name of your game.

Roll up! Roll up! Horoscopes galore!

ON FINISHING THE GIG, THE TEENAGERS GO UP TO THE STAR-SIGNS.

MARVIN REQUESTS HIS HOROSCOPE FROM STAR SIGN **'CAPRICORN'**:

CAPRICORN: You will reach the stars.

MARVIN: *(Puzzled)*
Ain't I reached them, already?

ANDREW REQUESTS HIS HOROSCOPE FROM STAR SIGN **'SAGITTARIUS'.**

SAGITTARIUS: You will achieve your ambition.

ANDREW: *(Excitedly)*
It's to be an actor and play the part of Romeo in Shakespeare's 'Romeo and Juliet'.

LANA: *(Frowning)*
You'll have to do a lot better than your last performance, Andrew.

DENZIL: What's your star sign, Jade?

JADE: Aquarius. Why?

DENZIL: Some star signs are meant for each other.

JADE: *(Looking dreamily at Denzil)*
Oh, right!

DENZIL SHYLY CLAMS UP.

JADE LOOKS CRESTFALLEN.

LANA: *(Whispers)*
He's saving his breath for his saxophone.

PETE: I don't believe in this horoscopes stuff. Sounds fishy to me.

JADE: What's *your* birth sign?

PETE: Pisces.

JADE: That's the 'fish'.
(Giggling)
You're thinking like a fish.

CANDIOLLA ARRIVES ON THE SCENE AND CONSULTS HER STAR SIGN – **'GEMINI'.**

GEMINI TWINS:	*(In one voice)* You must choose between two lovers.
CANDIOLLA:	*(Puzzled)* Two? Is God Anchises one of them?
GEMINI TWINS:	*(In one voice)* He is - and he isn't.
CANDIOLLA:	*(Petulantly)* You talk in riddles!

Cut to

ENTRANCE TO 'MOON ROLLOVER'

TRUNKA ENTERS, THE GOLDEN FLEECE DRAPED OVER HIS ARM.

HUMP HURRIES UP TO HIM.

HUMP:	I see you've got the Golden Fleece. Well done, Trunka!
TRUNKA:	Yeah! It's yours for 'Umpteen Sponduliks'.
HUMP:	That's pricey!
TRUNKA:	I want to settle down and open an 'Antique Bizarre'. All this travelling is keeping me away from my Missus - it's affecting our 'Elephantile'.

PIED PIPER HURRIES UP TO TRUNKA AND WITHOUT A 'BY YOUR LEAVE' GRABS THE FLEECE FROM HIM AND DRAPES IT OVER HIS SHOULDERS.

PIED PIPER:	*(Loudly)* I wish to be the spitting image of God Anchises'.
	NOTHING HAPPENS.
HUMP:	Maybe you should spit.
RAM:	Baaah! First say, *'Quickchange me'*.

WE GO WITH CANDIOLLA WHO IS SITTING BY HERSELF.

PIED PIPER, THE IMAGE OF GOD ANCHISES, GOES DOWN ON ONE KNEE BEFORE HER.

PIED PIPER: Candiolla, I have always loved you.

CANDIOLLA: *(Coyly)*
I find your declaration of love hard to believe Anchises.
You have the reputation of being a flirt.

PIED PIPER: *(Fervently)*
I only have eyes for you, Candiolla.

THE **REAL GOD ANCHISES** ARRIVES ON THE SCENE AND LOOKS DISBELIEVINGLY AT HIS MIRROR-IMAGE KNEELING BEFORE CANDIOLLA.

HE HURRIES OVER TO PIED PIPER.

ANCHISES: You're the image of me, but you can't be me! So who are you?

PIED PIPER: Your twin! We were separated at birth.

GOD ANCHISES: No-one ever told me I had a twin.

PIED PIPER IS BEGINNING TO CHANGE BACK INTO HIS OWN SELF. FIRST OF ALL THE LONG CAP AND TASSLE, AND THEN HIS PUCKISH FACE.

CANDIOLLA: *(Screams)*
Pied Piper, you wretch!

ANCHISES LEVELS A FIST AT PIED PIPER, WHO DUCKS AND RUNS.

THE GOLDEN FLEECE DRAPED ACROSS PIED PIPER'S SHOULDERS FALLS TO THE GROUND.

ANDREW, WHO IS IN THE VICINITY, SEES THE GOLDEN FLEECE FALL FROM PIED PIPER'S SHOULDERS, PICKS IT UP, RUNS AFTER HIM AND OFFERS BACK THE FLEECE.

PIED PIPER: *(Thrusting the fleece away)*
Put that fleece on, wish to be someone else and you've got yourself double-trouble!

                         HE HURRIES OFF.

ANDREW DRAPES THE GOLDEN FLEECE OVER HIS SHOULDERS.

ANDREW: I wish to be Romeo, from Shakespeare's drama, 'Romeo and Juliet'.

                         NOTHING HAPPENS.

RAM: Baaah! Say 'Quickchange me'.

ANDREW APPEARS BEFORE LANA.

SHE LOOKS ADMIRINGLY AT THE HANDSOME YOUNG MAN STANDING BEFORE HER
WEARING THE GARMENTS OF A YOUNG ITALIAN NOBLEMAN.

LANA: Wicked!

ANDREW: (Passionately)
                        Sweet Juliet, I am your Romeo!

LANA: THRILLED BY HIS WORDS - QUOTES EMOTIONALLY
                        FROM SHAKESPEARE'S DRAMA.

                        'Romeo, Romeo, wherefore art thou, Romeo?
                        Deny thy father, and refuse thy name;'

ANDREW: (Lightly)
                        I'll not be Romeo - I'll be Andrew, and we'll chill-out
                        together.

LANA STARES DISBELIEVINGLY AS ANDREW CHANGES BACK INTO HIS OWN SELF,
ON HIS FACE A BIG GRIN.

LANA: (Shrieks)
                        You! You - -

RAM: Baaah! Want me to butt his butt with my horns?

                        ANDREW FLEES.

Cut to
GAMING TABLE

SITTING AROUND A LARGE TABLE DOMINATED BY A **ROULETTE WHEEL**, ARE THE
GODS AND GODDESSES FROM MYTHOLOGY: THE **RED DRAGON:** AND **TANGLER
NED.** STANDING BESIDE THE LATTER IS ANOTHER TANGLER WHO IS HOLDING
THE CROCK OF GOLD.

HUMP: (Squeals)
                        Place your bets, now.

TANGLER NED: I'm going for Mars!

                      HE DIPS HIS HOOF INTO THE CROCK.

RED DRAGON: Is that the crock of gold from the maze at the end of
                      the rainbow?

TANGLER NED: It sure is!

RED DRAGON: I was told there was nothing in the crock.

TANGLER NED: There's enough gold in this crock to gamble millennium
                      nights away!

TRUNKA COMES INTO SIGHT.

RED DRAGON: You cheating elephant! You said the crock had nothing
                      in it.
                      (Pointing at the crock)
                      It's brimming with gold! - Give me back the Golden
                      Fleece, or I'll roast you alive!

TRUNKA: We did a deal - I gave you my clobber in exchange!

RED DRAGON SPILLS THE CONTENTS FROM THE SACK ONTO THE GROUND.

RED DRAGON: Lumps of worthless rock.

TRUNKA FLEES, FOLLOWED BY RED DRAGON, SPITTING FLAMES.

THERE IS AN EAR-SPLITTING ROLL OF THUNDER.

THE SORCERER COMES INTO VIEW. HE WAVES A WAND AT THE TANGLERS. - THEY
AND THE CROCK OF GOLD VANISH FROM THE TABLE.

Cut to
GALAXY

THE TANGLERS ARE HARNESSED TO A CHARIOT THAT HAS IN IT THE CROCK OF
GOLD.

THE SORCERER IS FEROCIOUSLY LASHING THE TANGLERS INTO A FAST GALLOP
WITH A MULTI-THONGED WHIP; THEIR BACKS ARE BADLY BLOODIED AND THEY
NEIGH IN AGONY.

FADE OUT

TAKE 18

Return to Hamelin

FADE IN

SPACESHIP

IT LANDS OUTSIDE THE 'MOON ROLLOVER'.

> ESH: *(To the children)*
> I must leave you for a while. There are jobs I have to do for the Sorcerer.

WAVING GOODBYE TO ESH, THE CHILDREN ENTER THE 'MOON ROLLOVER'.

THEY COME IN SIGHT OF A LARGE CAGE – IN IT ARE THE ABDUCTED CHILDREN.

> ISOLDA: They're not the children from Hamelin.

> JAMES: Our lot!

> HE POINTS AT GEMMA WHO IS POKING OUT HER TONGUE AT HIM.

> My sister.

THE CHILDREN WALK ON AND COME IN SIGHT OF THE **CHILDREN OF HAMELIN** CARRYING OUT CHORES:

TRISTAN AND ISOLDA HURRY UP TO THEM AND THERE ARE HUGS ALL ROUND.

THE FOUR CHILDREN SETTLE THEMSELVES IN A SECLUDED CORNER.

TRISTAN LEAFS THROUGH THE *'CENTURIES TIMETABLE'.*

BEN HOLDS THE POCKET WATCH, PREPARED TO WIND IT.

> TRISTAN: *'One, two, it's all so new'*

BEN WINDS THE WATCH. NOTHING HAPPENS.

> TRISTAN: *'Three, four - try some more'*

BEN AGAIN WINDS THE WATCH.

TRISTAN: 'Five, six - add a trick'

BEN: What's that supposed to mean?

TRISTAN SHAKES HIS HEAD.

JAMES: Change hands! Give the watch to me.

BEN DOES SO.

TRISTAN: 'Seven, eight - don't be late'

JAMES: I'm winding as fast as I can.

TRISTAN: 'Nine, ten!' – Back again!

THE WATCH GLEAMS BRIGHTLY AND THERE IS A FLASH:

WHEN THE FLASH CLEARS TRISTAN AND ISOLDA HAVE VANISHED, ALONG WITH THE CHILDREN OF HAMELIN; THE BROOMS, BRUSHES, AND PANS LEFT LYING AROUND, THE ONLY PROOF THAT THEY WERE EVER THERE.

Cut to

WOOD ON THE OUTSKIRTS OF HAMELIN

A WOODCUTTER IS CHOPPING WOOD IN FRONT OF A TUMBLEDOWN SHACK.

CANDIOLLA, HIS BEAUTIFUL GOLDEN-HAIRED DAUGHTER, COMES INTO VIEW.

SHE IS WALKING VERY SLOWLY SO AS NOT TO SPILL THE WATER IN THE PAILS, ONE AT EACH END OF THE STAVE THAT IS SLUNG ACROSS HER SHOULDERS.

HER CLOTHES ARE RAGGED. HER FEET ARE BARE.

PIED PIPER ARRIVES ON THE SCENE. HE REMOVES THE STAVE AND BUCKETS FROM CANDIOLLA'S SHOULDERS.

PIED PIPER: (Implores)
                            Marry me Candiolla. I'm dying of love for you.

CANDIOLLA: You're only a Pied Piper. I shall only marry a rich man who can give me fine clothes, jewels and a grand house.

THE **TOWN CRIER OF HAMELIN** COMES INTO VIEW RINGING A BELL AND ANNOUNCING IN A LOUD SONOROUS VOICE:

TOWN CRIER: ***HEAR YE! HEAR YE!***
THE CITIZENS OF HAMELIN
WILL PAY ONE THOUSAND GUILDERS
TO ANYONE WHO CAN RID THE CITY
OF THE RATS!

PIED PIPER: If I had one thousand Guilders, Candiolla, would you then marry me?

CANDIOLLA'S REPLY IS A WHIMSICAL SMILE.

Cut to
CITY HALL - HAMELIN

PIED PIPER IS STANDING BEFORE THE MAYOR.

MAYOR: *(Scornfully)*
How is it possible for a lowly Pied Piper to rid our city of the rats?

PIED PIPER: Assemble the citizens in the market place and I will show you.

Cut to
MARKET PLACE

THE MAYOR AND THE CITIZENS OF HAMELIN ARE GATHERED.

PIED PIPER ARRIVES ON THE SCENE.

CITIZEN: What jiggery-pokery are you up to, Pied Piper?

OTHER CITIZENS ADD THEIR GUFFAWS.

PIED PIPER PUTS HIS FLUTE TO HIS LIPS:

THE FIRST NOTES ARE SOFTLY LILTING THEN BECOME LOUDER AND LIVELIER.

PIED PIPER BEGINS JIGGING ON THE SPOT IN TIME TO THE FLUTE'S NOTES.

RATS, ALL SHAPES COLOURS AND SIZES, FROM EVERY CORNER OF HAMELIN, TUMBLE ONTO THE SCENE.

THE CITIZENS RECOIL HORROR-STRUCK!

PIED PIPER JIGS AWAY FROM THE MARKET PLACE, THE RATS SCAMPERING AFTER HIM IN A MESMERISED HORDE.

Cut to
RIVER BANK

PIED PIPER JIGS ALONG THE BANK AND THE RATS UNABLE TO HALT THEIR MAD SCAMPERING PLUNGE INTO THE RIVER, PILE UPON PILE, IN A STRUGGLING SQUEAKING MASS. THEY SINK BELOW THE SURFACE OF THE RIVER UNTIL AT LAST, THERE IS NOT A RAT TO BE SEEN.

Cut to
MARKET PLACE

THE CITIZENS AND THE RETURNED CHILDREN ARE HOLDING HANDS AND DANCING FOR JOY.

Cut to
CITY HALL

PIED PIPER PRESENTS HIMSELF BEFORE THE MAYOR WHO MEEKLY HANDS OVER THE MONEYBAG.

Cut to
WOOD

PIED PIPER IS KNEELING BEFORE CANDIOLLA, THE MONEYBAG AT HER FEET.

> PIED PIPER: I'm rich, Candiolla, I have one thousand Guilders. Will you now marry me?
>
> CANDIOLLA: *(Wistfully)*
> I'm a poor woodcutter's daughter and if I marry you I shall be a Pied Piper's wife. I wish to be nothing less than a Princess, so I shall await my Prince Charming.

FADE OUT

TAKE 19

A sit-down strike

FADE IN

'MOON ROLLOVER'

HUMP IS LOOKING DISMAYED AT THE BRUSHES, BROOMS, BUCKETS AND MOPS LEFT LYING AROUND BY THE CHILDREN OF HAMELIN.

HE SQUEALS HYSTERICALLY FOR PIED PIPER, WHO ARRIVES ON THE SCENE.

HUMP:	Where have the children of Hamelin gone?
PIED PIPER:	Their time here was up.
HUMP:	*(Wobbling in temper)* It had better not happen with this new lot!
	HE WOBBLES OVER TO WHERE THE CHILDREN ARE WORKING.

GEMMA TOSSES AWAY THE BROOM IN HER HAND AND STANDS SQUARELY IN FRONT OF HUMP, HER FACE SCOWLING, HANDS ON HER HIPS.

GEMMA:	How much are you going to pay us?
HUMP:	*(Taken aback)* Nothing! You're my slaves.

KATHY STANDS BESIDE GEMMA AND WAGS HER FINGER AT HUMP.

KATHY:	It's not nice to make children your slaves.
HUMP:	Nice, or, not nice, that's what you are.
GEMMA:	*(Firmly)* I'm not working for nothing.

GEMMA SITS DOWN ON THE GROUND, HER ARMS FOLDED AND GLARES AT HUMP.

ALL THE OTHER CHILDREN IMITATE GEMMA BY SITTING ON THE FLOOR, THEIR ARMS FOLDED.

HUMP CAN'T BELIEVE WHAT HE IS SEEING.

HUMP:	*(Squealing)* The children of Hamelin never behaved like this! *(To Gemma)* What is your name?
GEMMA:	Iron Kid.
KATHY:	She's a chip off the 'Iron lady'.
HUMP:	*(Squeals)* O ooh! – I've heard of her! She was the Prime Minister of Britain.

THE TWO GIRLS VIGOROUSLY NOD THEIR HEADS.

HUMP WHIRLS ABOUT PONDERING.

	One Planet Mars Bar, per head?
GEMMA:	*(Shakes her head)* Money please?
HUMP:	The only use for money in my Moon Rollover is for gambling.
KATHY:	*(Primly)* We don't want to get into bad ways, Gemma.
GEMMA:	*(Scowling)* Okay! The Planet Mars Bars.
KATHY:	*(To Hump)* Will there be extra for overtime?
GEMMA:	*(Shrieks)* There's no way we're working overtime, Kathy! This job is killing!

FADE OUT

TAKE 20

Exodus

FADE IN

EXT: MOON ROLLOVER

ANDREW, MARVIN, PETE, DENZIL AND TERRY, JAMES AND BEN ARE SHOVELLING SNOW AWAY FROM THE ENTRANCE TO THE 'MOON ROLLOVER'.

THE MOONMIFS COME INTO SIGHT FLYING OVERHEAD.

THEY LAND.

    BEN: *(Overjoyed)*
                      Your wing is all healed, Mookina!

    MOOKINA: Yes my dear! And we Moonmifs are going to help you and your friends escape from Planet Moona. - CLOUD NINE is waiting to carry you all away.

Cut to
INT: MOON ROLLOVER

THE TEENAGERS ARE QUIETLY ASSEMBLING THE CHILDREN TOGETHER.

    JAMES: *(Whispers to Gemma)*
                    We're leaving here!

    GEMMA: *(Crossly)*
                    We haven't been paid yet!

    JAMES: *(Scowling)*
                    You can stay if you like.

THE CHILDREN, NOW GATHERED INTO A SQUAD, ARE BEING SHEPHERDED OUT OF THE 'MOON ROLLOVER' BY THE TEENAGERS.

HUMP ARRIVES ON THE SCENE JUST AS THE TAIL-END OF THE SQUAD IS EXITING.

    HUMP: *(Squeals hysterically)*
                    Pied Piper! Pied Piper!

PIED PIPER APPEARS PLAYING HIS FLUTE AND JIGGING.

THE CHILDREN TURN AROUND AND JIG BACK INTO THE MOON ROLLOVER.

MOOKIN FLIES UP TO PIED PIPER AND PECKS HIS FINGERS SO THAT HE DROPS THE FLUTE. MOOKIN THEN FLIES OFF WITH IT IN HIS BEAK.

HUMP IS ROUGHLY PUSHING THE CHILDREN BACK INTO THE 'MOON ROLLOVER'.

MOOKINA AND OTHER MOONMIFS PECK ALL OVER HIM.

> HUMP: *(Squeals)*
> Help, I'm losing slime!

Cut to
CLOUD NINE

A LARGE FLUFFY CLOUD FLOATS TO GROUND LEVEL.

EVERYONE BOARDS THE CLOUD.

THE CLOUDS RISES AND FLOATS AWAY.

THE CHILDREN LIE SPRAWLED ON THE CLOUD AS THOUGH IT IS A DOWNY BED.

THE SUN BEGINS TO RISE ABOVE THE CURTAIN OF NIGHT AND THE CLOUD MELTS.

THE CHILDREN SCREAM TERRIFIED AS IT DISINTEGRATES, BUT INSTEAD OF FALLING, THEY FLOAT GENTLY DOWNWARDS AND LAND ON A LUSH GREEN PLAIN.

Cut to
LAND OF PLENTY

EXOTIC FRUITS HANG FROM THE TREES AND THERE ARE BUBBLING STREAMS.

THE CHILDREN PICK THE FRUIT AND QUENCH THEIR THIRST IN THE STREAMS, CUPPING THE WATER IN THEIR HANDS.

THE TEENAGERS LAUNCH INTO A GIG, LED BY MARVIN:

> *'We've travelled dreamtime,*
> *Seen fantastical climes.*
> *Had eyefuls of stars,*
> *Been neighbours to Mars.*

This is a fairyland for sure,
Bubbling streams, and fruits galore.
A flower-scented breeze,
Birds tweeting in the trees.

All's well while the sun is bright,
But who'll tuck us up tonight?
However far we may roam,
Ain't no place like HOME SWEET HOME!'

THERE IS THE SOUND OF THUNDERING HOOVES.

A CHARIOT PULLED ALONG BY TANGLERS COMES INTO VIEW.

HUMP IS SITTING IN THE CHARIOT, ALONGSIDE IT GALLOPS TANGLER NED, AND OTHER TANGLERS GALLOP BEHIND THE CHARIOT.

LASSOES WHIRL AND THE CHILDREN RUN WILDLY ABOUT SCREAMING AS THEY TRY TO AVOID BEING LASSOED.

THE MOONMIFS COME INTO VIEW FLYING OVERHEAD.

MOOKIN PECKS THE POUCH OF SEEDS HANGING FROM MOOKINA'S BEAK.

AS EACH SEED HITS THE GROUND, THERE SPRINGS UP IN ITS PLACE A **WARRIOR, HOLDING A SWORD AND SHIELD.** BEFORE LONG THERE IS A LARGE ARMY OF WARRIORS. THEY SET ABOUT SLAUGHTERING THE TANGLERS.

HUMP JUMPS ONTO THE BACK OF TANGLER NED WHO GALLOPS OFF AT A TERRIFIC SPEED AND THE TWO ARE SOON LOST TO SIGHT.

THE WARRIORS, HAVING SLAUGHTERED THE TANGLERS, MARCH AWAY IN A BAND FROM THE SCENE.

    ANDREW: *(To the others)*
                      So where do we go from here?

MOOKINA FLIES UP AND FLUTTERS A WING TOWARDS A MOUNTAIN IN THE DISTANCE.

    MOOKINA: Climb that mountain and on the other side of it you will
                      find Argos the boat builder. He will help you.

FADE OUT

TAKE 21

A Mountain of trouble

FADE IN

A MOUNTAIN

FLUFFY CLOUDS ENCIRCLE THE MOUNTAIN'S PEAK THAT IS TINGED WITH GOLD IN THE SUNLIGHT.

THEY ALL TREAD A PATH UP THE MOUNTAIN THAT TAKES THEM HIGHER AND HIGHER.

ALL THE WAY ALONG THE PATH, THE LONG TENDRILS OF HIDEOUS PLANTS CLUTCH AT THE CHILDREN AND OUT OF THE BUSHES CRAWL STUMPY CREATURES THAT STAND IN THEIR WAY.

THE TEENAGERS RUSH THE CREATURES, STAMPING THEIR FEET AT THEM, AND SHOUTING.

Cut to
NIGHTFALL

THE CHILDREN ARE HUDDLED TOGETHER ON THE GROUND TRYING TO SLEEP.

MONSTROUS SHAPES FLIT ABOUT MUTTERING AND LUMINOUS EYES GLEAM IN THE DARKNESS.

MARVIN STRUMS HIS GUITAR AND SINGS.

> *'Hey! Hey!*
> *Devils of the night*
> *Giving kids the fright!*
> *Save your ravings,*
> *Until dawn.'*

THE SHADOWY SHAPES CLUTCH AT HIM.

> *'Hey! Hey!*
> *Devils of the night,*
> *Quit your witchy spite!*
> *Your flair to scare,*
> *Ain't fair!'*

THE MURKY CLOUDS IN THE NIGHT SKY FADE AWAY TO REVEAL A BRIGHTLY SHINING FULL MOON THAT HAS A KINDLY FEMALE FACE.

MARVIN SINGS TO THE MOON:

> *'Hey! Hey!*
> *Clare de Lune.*
> *Be a 'Mother Moon'*
> *Wrap us in your 'Silver Shoon'*
> *All through the night.'*

THE MOON'S FACE BREAKS INTO A WIDE SMILE.

THE HORRIBLE MUTTERINGS CEASE: THE LUMINOUS EYES DISAPPEAR.

THE CHILDREN REST THEIR HEADS ON THEIR HANDS, AND ARE SOON FAST ASLEEP.

FADE OUT

TAKE 22

All aboard

FADE IN

ARGOS AND THE ARGONAUTS

THE CHILDREN AWAKE TO A GOLDEN DAWN.

DOWN BELOW, SPARKLING IN THE SUNLIGHT, IS AN EMERALD SEA, ITS GENTLE WAVES CURL TOWARDS THE SHORE, SPLASHING FROTHY FRINGES ONTO THE SAND.

THE CHILDREN DESCEND THE MOUNTAIN WITHOUT ANY FURTHER MISHAPS.

Cut to
SHORE

BUSILY WORKING ON THE FRAMEWORK OF A SHIP IS **ARGOS,** THE BOAT BUILDER FROM MYTHOLOGY.

ANDREW GOES UP TO ARGOS.

>ANDREW: Would you have a boat to spare, Sir?

ARGOS SMILINGLY LEADS ANDREW TO A BOAT THAT HAS **ARGONAUTS** SITTING AT ITS OARS.

EVERYONE BOARDS.

Cut to
CLIFFS OF COLCHIS

THE ARGONAUTS ARE VIGOROUSLY ROWING THE BOAT ON THE SEA.

AHEAD OF THEM, RISING UP FROM THE SEA, ARE TWO TOWERING CLIFFS OF ROCK.

ALL AROUND THE ROCKS ARE **WRECKED SHIPS.**

>ARGONAUT: *(Shouting fearfully)*
>The cliffs of Colchis! They crush to bits vessels that attempt to sail between them.

MOOKINA AND MOOKIN COME INTO VIEW FLYING OVERHEAD.

>THEY MEW TO THE ARGONAUTS:

>>***FOLLOW OUR FLIGHT, ARGONAUTS AND WHEN THE CLIFFS OPEN, LEAN SWIFTLY ON YOUR OARS.***

THE BOAT IS ROWED UP TO THE OPEN ROCKS.

THE ROCKS OPEN; MOOKINA AND MOOKIN FLY BETWEEN THEM AND THE ROCKS CRASH TOGETHER SCRAPING THE BIRD'S BODIES, THEIR FEATHERS FLY. - ON THE REBOUND THE ROCKS OPEN AGAIN -

MARVIN HAS ELECTED HIMSELF 'COX'.

MARVIN: (Shouts)
                           Trinidad and Tobago

THE ARGONAUTS STRAIN ON THEIR OARS AND THE BOAT LEAPS BETWEEN THE OPEN ROCKS BEFORE THEY CRASH TOGETHER AGAIN.

CHILDREN: Hurrah!

ARGONAUT: From now on, the rocks will forever stand still as it is
                           decreed that once a vessel sails safely between them,
                           they may never move again.

THE BOAT IS LANDED AND THE CHILDREN DISEMBARK.

THE MUTILATED BODIES OF MOOKINA AND MOOKIN LIE DEAD ON THE BEACH.

BEN: (Tearfully)
                           They gave their lives to save us.

MEWING IS HEARD FROM ABOVE.

THE CHILDREN LOOK UP AT THE SKY.

TWO BEAUTIFUL WHITE DOVES ARE FLYING TOGETHER.

THE VOICES OF MOOKINA AND MOOKIN MEW:

THE POWER OF LOVE! — THE POWER OF LOVE!

FADE OUT

TAKE 23

A journey through time

FADE IN

BEACH

JAMES IS LEAFING THROUGH THE *'CENTURIES TIME TABLE'*, WATCHED BY BEN, KATHY AND GEMMA.

JAMES:

If I could find the right numeral on the pocket watch to return us to Earth.

BEN:

I'll wind the watch anyway and see what happens.

BEN WINDS THE WATCH.

IT FLASHES.

Cut to
A GRASSY PLAIN

ERECTED ON IT, A SINGLE STONE HUT.

THE CHILDREN GO INSIDE AND SEE AN **OLD WOMAN.** GREY HAIR STRAGGLES TO HER SHOULDERS. HER DRESS IS ROUGH SACKING.

SHE IS VIGOROUSLY PUNCHING INTO WAKEFULNESS A **MAN ASLEEP IN A CHAIR.** ON HIS HEAD IS A SLIM CORONET OF IVY LEAVES AND WRAPPED AROUND HIM A CAPE.

THE MAN STIRS, OPENS HIS EYES AND LOOKS WITH DISMAY AT THE DISH OF BLACKENED CAKES RESTING ON HOT EMBERS.

OLD WOMAN:

(Shrieking)
I asked you to watch my cakes, you fell asleep and now they are all burnt!

JAMES READS FROM THE *'CENTURIES TIME TABLE'*.

'King Alfred the Great – 849'

(He offers the book to the king)
Would you care to leave a few words for posterity, Sir?

| KING ALFRED: | *(Sighing)*
Hell hath no fury like a Woman's Scorn |

BEN WINDS THE WATCH.

IT FLASHES.

Cut to
BANQUETING HALL

A BIG FAT MAN, A CROWN ON HIS HEAD, IS MUNCHING CHICKEN LEGS AND THROWING THE BONES OVER HIS SHOULDER.

JAMES READS FROM THE BOOK:

'King Henry V111 - 1457'

JAMES:	*(Disgustedly)* His mouth's too full to speak.
KATHY:	*(Primly)* He had six wives.
JAMES:	*(To Kathy)* *I'm* the faithful type.
	THEY GRIN AT EACH OTHER.
GEMMA:	*(Scowling)* I don't know what you see in my brother, Kathy — he's a pain.
JAMES:	There's Anne Boleyn sitting beside the king.
	HE GOES UP TO HER AND OFFERS THE OPEN BOOK.
	Would you care to leave a few words for posterity, Madam?
ANNE BOLEYN:	*(Sadly)* I lost my head.

BEN WINDS THE WATCH.

IT FLASHES.

Cut to
SEA SHORE

WE GO WITH A WOMAN WHO HAS A NOBLE POINTED FACE. ON HER RED
ELABORATELY STYLED HAIR SITS A CROWN SPARKLING WITH DIAMONDS. HER
DRESS IS ENCRUSTED WITH JEWELS. ON EACH FINGER OF HER DELICATE HANDS,
IS A RING OF FINE GEMS.

SHE IS WAVING TO THE SHIPS ON THE SEA.

JAMES READS FROM THE BOOK:

'Queen Elizabeth First of England – 1533'

HE BOWS LOW TO THE QUEEN, THEN OFFERS HER THE
OPEN BOOK.

Would you care to leave a few words for posterity, Your
Majesty?

QUEEN: *I have the body of a weak and feeble woman - but I
have the heart and stomach of a man!'*

JAMES AGAIN BOWS LOW, THEN WITHDRAWS.

GEMMA: *(Wrinkling her nose)*
How can she have the 'heart and stomach of a man'?

JAMES: *(Smugly)*
The Queen is saying, 'She's brave like us men.'

GEMMA: *(Grimaces)*
Ugh!

BEN WINDS THE WATCH.

IT FLASHES.

Cut to
A DARK CELLAR

A MAN WEARING A THREE-CORNERED HAT AND CLOAK IS MOVING BARRELS.
AROUND.

SOLDIERS ENTER.

CAPTAIN: *(To the man)*
                     We arrest you in the name of King James First of
                     England.

JAMES READS FROM THE BOOK:

                     **'Guido Fawkes - Gunpowder Plot, 5th November
                     1605.'**

                     HE HURRIES AFTER GUY FAWKES WHO IS BEING
                     ROUGHLY LED AWAY BY THE SOLDIERS.

                     Would you care to leave a few words for posterity, Sir?

GUY FAWKES: *(Mournfully)*
                     The best-laid fireworks go awry!

BEN WINDS THE WATCH.

IT FLASHES.

Cut to
WINDSOR CASTLE

A PORTLY LADY DRESSED SEVERELY IN BLACK, A CROWN ON HER HEAD, IS
SITTING AT A TABLE THAT HAS ON IT A DELICATE PORCELAIN CHINA TEA SET —
WITH ONLY TWO CUPS AND SAUCERS. SHE IS POURING TEA FROM THE SILVER
JUG IN HER HAND INTO THE CUPS.

                     JAMES READS FROM THE BOOK.

                     'Queen Victoria — 1819'

                     BOWING LOW, JAMES OFFERS THE QUEEN THE OPEN
                     BOOK.

                     Would you care to leave a few words for posterity, Your
                     Majesty?

QUEEN VICTORIA: *A nice cup of tea, not too weak and not too strong,*
                     brewed from a fine Colonial blend.

GEMMA GETS VERY CLOSE TO THE TABLE AND THE CUP OF TEA SPILLS OVER.

QUEEN VICTORIA: *(Crossly)*
                     You clumsy child!

A WICKED EXPRESSION COMES OVER GEMMA'S FACE: SHE POINTS TO UNDER THE CHAIR ON WHICH THE QUEEN IS SITTING.

GEMMA: *(Pointing)*
There's a mouse under your chair.

QUEEN: *(Jumps up shrieking)*
A MOUSE!

SHE RUNS FROM THE ROOM HOLDING UP HER SKIRTS.

BEN HASTILY WINDS THE WATCH.

IT FLASHES.

FADE OUT

TAKE 24

Home Sweet Home

FADE IN

SELESTRIA PLATFORM

THE FOUR CHILDREN ARE BACK WITH THE OTHER CHILDREN AND TEENAGERS ON THE PLATFORM.

ESH'S SPACESHIP COMES INTO SIGHT.

JAMES AND BEN SHOUT TOGETHER:

'ESH'

THE SHIP DROPS IN HEIGHT, A PATH OF LIGHT EXTENDS FROM IT TOWARDS JAMES AND BEN. THEY VANISH.

GEMMA: *(Shrieking)*
They've gone and left us behind!

KATHY: James will be back for us, Gemma!

GEMMA:	No he won't.
KATHY:	*(Dreamily)* I know he will.
GEMMA:	I don't know what you see in my brother – he's a –
	SHE STOPS ABRUPTLY KATHY HAVING PUT A FINGER TO GEMMA'S LIPS.

Cut to
INT: SHIP

BOYS TOGETHER:	Hi, ESH!
ESH:	*(Trills)* Hi!
JAMES:	It's great to see you again, ESH.
ESH:	There's not enough room in my ship to return everyone to Earth, so we're going to the Pole Star where Rudi-Reindeer, runs a sleigh service.

Cut to
POLE STAR

REINDEERS ARE PACKING SLEIGHS WITH ALL SORTS OF TOYS, AND PACKAGES.

ESH GOES UP TO A REINDEER THAT HAS MASSIVE HORNS AND AN EXCEPTIONALLY LARGE GLOWING RED NOSE.

ESH:	Hi, Rudi! How are you?
RUDI REINDEER:	Up the pole!
ESH:	Rudi, I'm hoping you can help out. Children abducted from Planet Earth by a Pied Piper are stranded on the Selestria Platform. Could you sleigh them back home?
RUDI REINDEER:	I haven't any sleighs to spare! They've all been taken by Santa Klaus to carry his goodies to Earth. It's Christmas Eve down there.

ESH: If you let the children down Rudi, *they* won't have a Christmas at all. - 'THE PETS' pop group also need a lift to get back in time for their Christmas Gig. If you help out, they'll sing a song about you and your red nose that could make it to 'Number One' in the Charts.

RUDI REINDEER: 'THE PETS' - Wow! Their beat really grabs me! - I'll see what I can do!

Cut to

NORTH LONDON

BELLS JINGLE AS THE SLEIGHS FULL OF CHILDREN FLY OVERHEAD, PULLED ALONG BY THE REINDEERS.

THE LOCALS FILL THE STREETS AND GAZE UP AT THE SKY.

THE SLEIGHS LAND AND THE CHILDREN RUN INTO THE ARMS OF THEIR PARENTS.

'THE PETS' gig, led by Marvin.

> *'Home! Sweet home!*
> *Ain't no place like home*
> *Wherever you may roam*
> *Near or far, reaching for a star,*
> *Crossin' land or sea,*
> *HOME'S the place to be.*
>
> *'It's hard to believe*
> *We're home for Christmas Eve*
> *We made it all the way*
> *On RUDI THE REINDEER'S SLEIGHS,*
> *For he's a jolly good fellah!*
> *HOORAH! HOORAH! HOORAH!'*

PARENTS AND CHILDREN CHORUS:

HURRAH! HURRAH!

RUDI AND THE OTHER REINDEERS PULL THE EMPTY SLEDGES HIGHER AND
HIGHER SKYWARDS AND DISAPPEAR BEYOND THE HORIZON.

Cut to
SPACESHIP

JAMES AND BEN ARE PREPARING TO LEAVE.

JAMES:	Will we ever see you again, ESH?
ESH:	Wherever there's trouble, you can depend on it.
BEN:	*(Sadly)* Bye, Man! I mean – mouse!
	THE THREE BRUSH HANDS AS BROTHERS'

Cut to
GROUNDS - PETUNIA HEIGHTS

BEN'S PARENTS, AND JAMES'S PARENTS, WITH THEM GEMMA, ARE LOOKING
ALL AROUND HOPING TO SIGHT JAMES AND BEN.

JOYCE PRINCE:	*(Anxiously)* Why wasn't my Ben with the other returned children?
GEMMA:	Him and James are never coming back.
JOHN BAINES:	Why do you say that, Gemma?
GEMMA:	They went off in the mouse's ship.
JOYCE PRINCE:	*(Tearfully to her husband)* Our only child.

WE GO WITH BEN RUNNING AT FULL SPEED TOWARDS HIS PARENTS.

BEN:	*(Shouting)* Mum! Dad!
	HE LEAPS INTO HIS MUM'S OPEN ARMS, HIS STURDY FRAME ALMOST KNOCKING HER OFF HER FEET.
	LLOYD PRINCE PUTS HIS ARMS AROUND BOTH OF THEM, BEAMING BROADLY.

JAMES STROLLS UP TO HIS PARENTS.

JAMES: Hi, Mum! Hi, Dad!

JOHN BAINES: *(Gruffly)*
                         Where on earth have you been, James?

JAMES REMOVES HIS SPECTACLES, WIPES THEM VERY DELIBERATELY WITH A HANDKERCHIEF, AND RETURNS THEM TO HIS NOSE.

JAMES: *(Smug smile on his face)*
                         Off the earth, dad, trailing the stars!

E N D

ONCE UPON A GALAXY

Cast of characters in order of appearance

Citizens of Hamelin
Pied Piper
Mayor
James Baines
Ben Prince
Mr Popov - Watch and clock repairer
Hump - Ruler Planet Moona
Pied Piper
Lloyd Prince - Father of Ben
John Baines - Father of James
Gemma Baines
ESH - 'Ever so Helpful' mouse
Kathy Murphy
Headmistress - Knowall Junior School
'THE PETS' POP GROUP
Andrew - plays guitar
Marvin - plays guitar – lead singer
Pete - plays keyboard
Denzil - plays saxophone
Terry - plays drums
Lana - dance backup
Jade - dance backup
Mookin – Moonmif
Mookina – Moonmif
Tanglers - Horses
Trunka Elephant -Tinker of the Galaxy
Red Dragon
Queen Medea
Cat soldiers
Parakeet
Ram – Golden Fleece
Tristan – boy from City of Hamelin
Isolda - girl from City of Hamelin
Queen Denderra
Candiolla
God Anchises
Horoscopes
Argos - Boatbuilder from Mythology
Argonauts
Characters from history -*Journey Through Time*
Rudi Reindeer
Parents of children

'IN THE PICTURE' FANTASIES
screenplay abbreviations

TAKE:
A scene.

EXT:
Exterior shot

INT:
Interior shot

CUT TO:
A quick transition from one scene to another, used when the action is continuous in time.

FADE IN:
Scene begins

FADE OUT:
Scene ends

CLOSE UP:
Used to enlarge a face or detail.

POV:
Point of view

OSV:
Voice over

SFX
Special effects

ZOOM:
Camera lens

SHOT:
Unit of action

CLAPPERBOARD:
Held in front of the camera to provide a visual record of the scene and take number.

DIRECTOR'S CAMERA TECHNIQUES:
The camera shots are the Director's choice. The screenwriter does not give directions in the script.

Recommended reading for aspiring film directors and writers:
'Writing for Television' – William Smethurst ISBN 1-85703-666-2
'Film Making' James Marsh ISBN 0-340-79163-2